ERROL
BROOME

Gracie
AND THE
emperor

ANNICK PRESS

TORONTO + NEW YORK + VANCOUVER

We acknowledge the support of the Canada Council for the Arts, the Ontario Arts Council, and the Government of Canada through the Book Publishing Industry Development Program (BPIDP) for our publishing activities.

Copy edited by Elizabeth McLean
Cover design and interior design by Irvin Cheung/iCheung Design
Cover illustration by Alisa Baldwin

First published in Australia by Allen and Unwin

The text was typeset in Bembo and Voluta Script

Cataloging in Publication
Broome, Errol
    Gracie and the emperor / written by Errol Broome. — North American ed.
ISBN 1-55037-891-0 (bound).—ISBN 1-55037-890-2 (pbk.)
    I. Title.
PZ7.B793Gr 2005   j823'.914   C2004-905982-3

Printed and bound in Canada

Published in the U.S.A. by   Distributed in Canada by: Distributed in the U.S.A. by:
Annick Press (U.S.) Ltd.   Firefly Books Ltd.   Firefly Books (U.S.) Inc.
                              66 Leek Crescent   P.O. Box 1338
                              Richmond Hill, ON   Ellicott Station
                              L4B 1H1   Buffalo, NY 14205

Visit our website at: **www.annickpress.com**

About Napoleon Bonaparte

NAPOLEON BONAPARTE was a brilliant soldier who rose to become Emperor of France. He waged war across Europe and became the most famous and feared man in the world. Napoleon won forty battles before his defeat at the Battle of Waterloo in 1815. Britain banished him to St. Helena, a remote island in the South Atlantic. There, he lived as a prisoner, surrounded by French courtiers and servants who accompanied him into exile and continued to treat him as their king. He died on St. Helena in 1821 at the age of fifty-two. An argument between his French court and the English governor, who refused to allow the name Napoleon on the grave unless Bonaparte was added, resulted in a headstone that simply read *Here lies...* Nineteen years later, his body was exhumed by the French and taken back to Paris to a hero's welcome.

For all the descendants of the Carew and Moss families of St. Helena.

Giant Bonaparte

FROM *The Mother Goose Treasury*
BY RAYMOND BRIGGS

Baby, baby, naughty baby,
Hush, you squalling thing, I say.
Peace this moment, peace, or maybe
Bonaparte will pass this way.

Baby, baby, he's a giant,
Tall and black as Rouen steeple,
And he breakfasts, dines, rely on't,
Every day on naughty people.

Baby, baby, if he hears you,
As he gallops past the house,
Limb from limb at once he'll tear you,
Just as pussy tears a mouse.

And he'll beat you, beat you, beat you
And he'll beat you all to pap,
And he'll eat you, eat you, eat you,
Every morsel snap, snap, snap.

October 17, 1815

"NO," SAID GRACIE, "I *WON'T* MAKE HIS BED!"

Mr. Porteous stared at her, his face white with shock. No working girl had ever spoken to him like this. His voice was slow and firm. "Bonaparte will be a guest here till a house is ready for him." He pointed towards a room at the top of the stairs. "Now make his bed!"

"Bonaparte kills people," muttered Gracie.

"Bonaparte is coming as a prisoner," said Mr. Porteous. "He can't hurt anyone now."

"People say he eats children," she said.

"Nonsense, child! Who's filled your head with such ideas?"

Gracie wasn't telling. She stared at the floorboards. "Everybody knows." As long as she could remember, her father had told her stories of Napoleon Bonaparte, who would stop at nothing to rule the world and plant the French flag on the Tower of London. Napoleon marched through country after country at the head of 600,000 troops. The mention of his name filled Gracie's head with images of swords and cannons and corpses piled high on the battlefields. Children in England went to bed afraid he'd come in the night to take them prisoner. He might even eat them! Over and over again, Gracie had pictured him in her mind, a huge, blustering man with hands like buckets, a leering face and teeth like a tiger.

Whenever Gracie whined about living here, on the remote island of St. Helena, her father said, "At least we're safe from Napoleon Bonaparte."

How could she ever believe anyone? And how could Mr. Porteous have Bonaparte here, in his boarding house? She turned to him, her cheeks tinged with red. "I can't believe you'd let him come!"

Mr. Porteous swallowed hard and jabbed at the air. "Go up there and make the bed this minute — *and don't come back tomorrow!*"

Gracie jerked her head to face him, but Mr. Porteous had already turned his back on her. She'd lost her job. What would she tell her father? Her first thought was to run away, right now, away from Mr. Porteous's boarding house, away from home, far from this island where she'd never wanted to be. But she had nowhere to go. Like Bonaparte, she was a prisoner here.

This desolate rock, flung far into the South Atlantic Ocean a week's sail from Africa, was held prisoner itself by battering winds and rain and an unrelenting sun. It was like a small ship stuck fast in the ocean. Its people weren't shipwrecked, but marooned so far from everywhere that the world didn't know they existed.

Gracie had read in books of other places in the world, where raspberries didn't come only in tins of jam, and apples grew on trees. Families picnicked on shady lawns and in the evening you could hear a bird, like a young girl singing.

How could Gracie ever know what other people saw and heard unless she could see and hear for herself? The rest of the world lay farther away than she could imagine. Some countries had neighbors; people traveled and visited other places St. Helena had no neighbors. It was itself like an exile.

Why would anyone want to live here? No one came by choice. Gracie was convinced her father had run away to St. Helena to escape troubles at home. He no longer spoke of England. Here, where he'd met her mother, was the only place he knew now, whether he liked it or not.

Gracie groaned. She couldn't leave without finishing the job. Angry red blotches stained her cheeks as she pulled clean sheets from the linen cupboard and burst into the small room that waited for Napoleon Bonaparte. She flung the sheets on the bed, then bent to unfold them and lay them out flat.

She lifted one corner of the mattress and slammed it down before tucking the sheet around the edges. How could the most famous, the most dreaded man in the world, be coming here, to the very place where she worked every afternoon?

When she'd finished, she looked back at the bed. She'd done a neat job, her last at Mr. Porteous's boarding house. Before she left the place for ever, she took a pen from the inkwell on a table beside the window and scribbled on a sheet of paper.

I made your bed, so there!

Now, let the cockroaches and bedbugs take over! Gracie stamped down the stairs and into the main street of Jamestown. She had nowhere to go. All because of Napoleon Bonaparte, who killed children.

The sun was fading fast, but she couldn't go home. She was afraid of her father's temper. Lately, he'd hardly spoken a kind word to her. Any small irritation, anything that went wrong, made him fly into a rage. When he heard she'd lost her job, he would lock her in her room above the shop without any dinner.

Samuel Taverner's shop had always struggled to make a profit. He and his wife had only scraped a living from the business. Now it was just him and Gracie, and they needed the few shillings she earned each week.

THIS EVENING THE STREETS OF JAMESTOWN were busier than she'd ever seen them. Gracie gasped as troops marched past, jerkily, like wound-up toy soldiers. The air was tight with tension. Something big was happening. Soldiers stood guard on every corner, and formed a solid line from the quay to the boarding house. All the people of the island had come into town and were gathering at the water's edge. As dusk closed in, their flaming torches lit patterns in the air.

Gracie dodged past her father's shop and mingled with the throng around the quay. Never had the port seen so many ships. The governor of St. Helena was waiting at the water's edge among a host of soldiers in uniform. Across the crowd, a flare lit up the faces of her friends Peggy and Jess. She raised her hand to wave, but the flare moved on, hiding them in the darkness.

Behind her, a small boy clutched his father's hand. "But what's it about?"

"Napoleon's coming," said the man.

"Who's Napoleon?"

"Freddie, I've *told* you."

"The scary one! Why do I have to see him?"

"Because everyone wants to see him—just to look at the man who almost ruled the world."

"So why's he here?"

"Because, Freddie, in the end he lost. The English beat him."

"But he's *here!* Why's he here?"

Gracie turned to listen. She, too, wanted to know, to try to understand how such a man could be thrust upon her small community.

"Because it's so far from anywhere. The English have sent him somewhere he'll never escape from, and there'll be no more battles."

"So will he be here till he dies?"

The man sighed. "I suppose so, Freddie, and that will be a very long time." He hoisted the boy onto his shoulders. "Just look now, and remember. Look! Look, he's coming!"

Gracie craned her neck as a small boat pulled into the wharf.

A hand grasped her elbow. "Hi, Gracie!"

"Hester!" Gracie spun around and grabbed her friend's hands. She didn't want to see this Bonaparte, yet she couldn't stop herself from looking.

"It's the Emperor!" cried a voice in the crowd.

"Oh, Gracie," said Hester. "He's just a man."

The man who had terrified millions walked up the cobbled steps from the jetty. He was surprisingly small. Even his cocked hat couldn't make him appear tall. He wore white breeches with high black boots, and a long green jacket, open to reveal a tight, round stomach.

If it hadn't been for the uniform, Gracie thought, he would have looked just like her father. Samuel was thinner, but not much taller, and they walked with the same purposeful stride. She even noticed the hands, small and pale like her father's.

A group of men and women stepped from a second boat and clustered around Bonaparte. They wore what seemed to Gracie like dress-up costume. Brilliant blue uniforms glinted with gold trim. Other men wore white knee breeches, stockings and shining buckled shoes, with long jackets and neckties like starched white table napkins. The women wore long gowns falling in soft folds from above the waist. Their shoulders were bare, and their hair twisted into coils entwined with jewels.

"Who *are* these people?" murmured Gracie.

"He's brought his court with him," said Hester. "Is it some kind of joke?"

Gracie shivered. "It's no joke."

People crushed to get a closer look. Their waving torches closed in around the official party. Guards clicked heels and cleared the way.

"He sleeps in a bed," Gracie whispered to Hester. "I made it up for him."

"Of course he sleeps in a bed. What do you think he is?"

"He's a monster. They say he eats three sheep for breakfast—and who knows what else! He wants to kill all English people."

"Pipe down, Gracie."

"How can I? People in England don't have to worry any more because they've sent him here—to us!"

Bonaparte and his party of French courtiers and servants were making their way through the line of troops towards the boarding house. The crowd began to break up, walking to their houses or to horses waiting drowsily to haul the farm carts home.

Gracie grasped her friend's arm. "Hester... I can't... I can't go home."

Hester peered into Gracie's dark almond eyes. "What's happened?"

"I've lost my job. Father will be furious. I don't know what to do."

"Then go straight home. Now, tell him now!"

"Hester, you know Father. Lately, I can't do a thing right. He's always picking on me. I can't face him—not today. I can't go home. Can I... do you think I could spend the night at your house?"

"All right, I'll ask. But what about clothes?"

Gracie gazed at her limp cotton dress. She had nothing else with her. "I can't go back, not yet."

"We'll find something," said Hester. "Come on, then, let's go."

2

OF COURSE, SAMUEL TAVERNER CAME LOOKING for
Gracie. She knew he would. It wouldn't take him long to walk
the few streets of Jamestown. He'd be banging on all the neighbors' doors.

In the dark of night, when the streets were quiet, and she
and Hester were together in the cramped single bed, she heard
his knock. "I'm not going," she whispered.

"Shh," said Hester. "Let Mum and Dad talk to him."

Gracie heard his voice, gruff, and without any hello or good
evening. "Have you seen Gracie?"

"Oh!" said Alice Kendrew. "I thought you knew. She's here
with us tonight."

"No!" he roared. "How was I supposed to know? That girl
has a will of her own."

"Let her be," said the woman. "It's late. I'll see she gets to
school tomorrow."

"You see she gets to work after school, too!"

"I told you!" whispered Gracie. "He'll never forgive me."

Hester reached for her hand. "Ssh!"

They lay still and listened.

"You look done in, Samuel," said William Kendrew. "Sit down and have a drink with us now."

Samuel Taverner sighed. "You've always been good to me, William—and to Gracie, too. It hasn't been easy for her. Some people don't like the slant of her eyes."

"You worry too much," said Alice.

"You know it's true. If you're half Chinese, you're only half English. Her mother was a good woman..."

Gracie sat up in bed. She liked—she longed—to hear people talk about her mother. Her father never spoke to Gracie of Rose. He kept his feelings bottled up, and if ever he opened the stopper all that poured out was anger. So Gracie held her silence, too. Rose had been sick for so long before she died, and the twelve months since then seemed half a lifetime.

Gracie fingered the smooth jade bracelet on her wrist, the bracelet Rose had worn always and promised to Gracie for her twelfth birthday. She'd given it, instead, the day Gracie turned ten, and Gracie knew, then, that Rose wouldn't be there to give it on her twelfth birthday.

Gracie wore the bracelet like a part of herself, and took it off only on bath day. It was all she had from her mother. Samuel had not thrown out or given away a single thing. Everything that belonged to Rose was locked in the wardrobe. Nobody could touch its contents, not even Gracie. Especially Gracie.

"We miss Rose, too," Alice said.

Everyone misses her, thought Gracie. She heard the grating of a chair on the floor, so close to the small bedroom that she ducked her head under the blanket. Someone sighed.

"So what am I expected to do?" said Samuel. "A man needs a woman to raise a child in this place."

"Come on, Samuel," said William. "Give yourself a break. Let us look after Gracie tonight."

"Everyone's stirred up this evening," said Alice. "It's been a big day. No one knows quite what to make of it. Whoever could have thought Napoleon Bonaparte would come here, to St. Helena!"

Gracie laid a hot cheek back on the pillow. She had a feeling St. Helena would never be the same again.

SHE HAD TO FIND ANOTHER JOB. Until she could bring in money, she couldn't go back to her father.

"Stay with us as long as you like," Hester said next morning.

Alice Kendrew smiled as the two girls ate breakfast. "I'll speak to your father," she said.

"It's no use," said Gracie. "He won't listen to anyone. I don't know what's wrong with him."

William laid his hand on her shoulder. Gracie stared up at him. "Why... do you know why?" She had a feeling he did.

"We talked sometimes, your father and I, especially when Rose was sick. I understand him, just a bit."

Gracie breathed a long sigh. "I wish I did."

"There's always been something bothering him, even before Rose became ill. I think it's... has he told you about your Uncle Isaac?"

"Nothing. Who's he?"

William frowned, and didn't reply.

"You have to tell me now."

"He's your father's twin brother."

"Twin! He never told me he had a twin—or even a brother."

"No one could believe they were twins. They weren't a bit alike. Isaac was tall and good at everything..."

"And Father wasn't!"

William coughed. "Perhaps he didn't think he was. I don't think they got along too well. Isaac was going to be a doctor. Your grandparents wanted Samuel to go into the army, but he hated the idea. He saw only one way of escape—and of getting out of his clever brother's shadow, so he left home."

"I knew there was something he wouldn't tell," said Gracie. "What happened to Isaac?"

"He went into the army."

"And Father didn't, he came here instead." She shrugged. "Well, I don't see why we can't talk about it." She sat up straight as thoughts strung together in her mind. "He isn't here now, is he? Isaac, with the soldiers?"

"You'll have to ask your father that. It's none of my business."

"An uncle!" mused Gracie. "I didn't know I had an uncle." Why would her father shut his brother out of his life? Gracie had noticed how edgy Samuel had become since ships started unloading soldiers on the island. Was he afraid he might meet his lost brother now, face to face? She didn't want to ask him. Probing would only inflame his wrath. She sat in the Kendrews' kitchen, staring at the wall.

"Sometimes Samuel finds it hard to cope," said William. "We like having you here—we'll keep you with us forever, if you give us Rose's recipe for wonton soup."

William Kendrew turned everything into a joke. No matter how difficult life became, he never complained about this island. Hester said he'd written dozens of letters hoping for work back in England. Each letter took sixty-seven days to get there on a sailing ship, and longer for a reply to come back. Gracie hoped there would never be a reply. She couldn't imagine St. Helena without Hester.

Jobs at the shipping yard came with the ships that called at the island. Sometimes William Kendrew went without work for days or even a week, but today the port had never been busier. The harbor was filled with ships. Nine extra vessels had come, bringing soldiers to guard Napoleon. "Bonaparte is putting pennies in our pockets," he said as he stuck a cap on his head and made for the door.

"I might be late tonight," said Gracie. "I'm going looking for a new job."

Alice Kendrew nodded, but Gracie saw the look of concern on her face. "If you must, you must."

"I need to do it today," said Gracie. Word spread quickly in Jamestown, and people would soon hear that Mr. Porteous had given her the sack. They'd whisper between themselves that she was a headstrong, difficult girl. It might be better to seek work outside the town, away from her father and away from the monster who had come into their midst.

AFTER SCHOOL THAT DAY, Gracie set out on foot, wearing the same faded cotton dress, and followed the treeless, rocky path that wound up the hill from Jamestown.

Being away from her father gave her time to think. She was afraid of his temper. Her mother had known how to calm him. "There now, Samuel," she'd say when she saw him simmering inside. "You're not to blame for anything."

"My Chinese medicine," she called it, but it was only words and a gentle hand on his arm. Rose understood him.

He was angry when she died, and felt deprived. Can't he understand that I'm deprived, too? thought Gracie.

Still, she had to admit, he'd tried. In those first few weeks, he wouldn't let Gracie out of his sight. "Stay with me, Gracie," he said over and over again, as if he were afraid of himself.

"Of course I will," she said.

And then, slowly, his mood turned. He niggled and complained. Gracie didn't cook as well as her mother did. How could a man manage a daughter on his own? She was growing out of all her clothes. He was sick of rats getting into everything. What if people stopped coming to the shop? Gracie would have to get work to help pay the bills.

Last week, when the fire in the grate went out, he'd blamed Gracie. He was busy in the shop. Why wasn't she there to see to it? "I was working at the boarding house," she said. "I can't be everywhere." To punish her, he locked her in her room above the shop. So he didn't have to look at her, she believed. I'm not *that* bad to look at, she told herself. Alice Kendrew said she had her mother's eyes: dark, glistening, almond-shaped pools. Others said she looked like her father, with the strong, determined chin of the English.

Some days she thought he was angry that she had her mother's eyes, that they belonged to Rose and only to Rose. At other times, she wondered if she'd turned out exactly like her mother, if he might have loved her more. Or could he be disappointed because she wasn't more like him? She'd never know. She was neither one thing nor the other and somehow she didn't fit comfortably into his life.

At times it seemed he almost hated her. And when she was shut in her room, she wondered if she hated him. There was a thin line between love and hate, and sometimes no line at all. One just seeped into the other when you weren't looking.

A wild goat huffed and darted across the track, but otherwise the country was silent. No birds sang. The path grew steeper and rougher. In places, not even a cactus sprouted from the barren hillside. No wonder they called this island The Rock.

Gracie passed small whitewashed houses on farms that eked out a living from a few scrawny cattle. It was no use asking these farmers for work.

On she walked for more than an hour. Evening was closing in when she came to the graceful white house called The Briars. The family who lived there kept a household of servants and sent their son to boarding school in England. Perhaps they had some extra job for a girl like Gracie. She took a deep breath and started up the avenue of banyan trees towards the house.

THROUGH THE TREES, she saw valets and maids scurrying between the big house and smaller timber building across the garden.

Five horses stood outside the stables. On the vast lawn, a gardener was cutting a motif in the grass. From where Gracie stood, it looked a bit like a crown. Was this a normal afternoon at The Briars? she wondered.

She followed one of the many paths towards the stables and spoke to the young groom. "Could you tell me where I'll find the housekeeper?"

The boy was a head taller than her, with a twist of rust-colored hair that hung over one eye like a question mark. He looked down on Gracie. "Mr. George is very busy today."

"I only want to ask..."

"He won't have time to talk to you." He pointed towards the house. "See, there he is now, with his knickers in a knot."

"Eh?" said Gracie. But she couldn't waste time asking questions. She ran along the path to the man who stood, signaling, as if he were directing traffic.

"Excuse me..."

The man waved her away. "What is it, girl?"

"I was wondering... would you... do you have work I could do?"

"We don't need any more servants. Don't bother me now."

"I'm no servant," she said.

He stood tall and peered down at her. "So? Really!"

In a corner of the green lawn, two girls older than Gracie were chasing their two small brothers. The girls wore sweeping skirts and frilled pantaloons to their ankles.

Gracie saw herself then as Mr. George might see her, thin and sallow-skinned, wearing a washed-out, creased cotton dress. What must he think of a poor girl like her? She shouldn't have had the cheek to come here.

She bowed her head and saw only Mr. George's shiny black shoes. Then she turned and walked away.

"Ahem." The man coughed. "Just a minute, child."

Gracie stopped.

"Come here. How old are you?"

"Eleven."

"Hmmm. We *are* rather busy at the moment. A VIP has come to stay, so we could use a little help today."

"I can make beds," she said.

"And clean up, wash dishes?"

"Oh, yes."

"Come, then." He led her around the side of the house to the back entrance.

Men's voices came from the building known as the Pavilion,

speaking in a language she didn't understand. Everything was foreign to her here.

Mr. George took her into the kitchen, a big room with an enormous table in the center. Steam from boilers and cooking pots billowed from both sides of the room. Maids in gray uniforms darted from table to stove with an air of bustle and importance. They took no notice of Gracie.

"Tonight, and until other arrangements can be made, the General will eat in the main house," said Mr. George. "Dinner will be served at nine o'clock. Your job begins when the guests have finished. So, do what Mrs. Pratt says."

Then he was gone.

A plump, ruddy-faced woman was suddenly beside Gracie. She was dressed in blue and white, like two cushions tied in the middle.

"What's your name, child?"

"Gracie."

"Well, Gracie, perhaps now you could fetch some water from the well outside." She leaned back and puffed herself out till the apron pulled tight across her chest. "It's not every day we have an emperor to dinner."

Gracie stared at Mrs. Pratt. It couldn't be! "Not Bonaparte?"

"Who else? He's asked to stop here."

Couldn't she ever get away from him? "But... but why?"

"Longwood House isn't ready yet. And this is a much nicer place for him than that old boarding house."

Mrs. Pratt hummed to herself and beamed at Gracie. "We haven't had anyone like this before. Soldiers, yes, and important visitors, but never an emperor."

"They call him General now."

"True." Mrs. Pratt wiped her hands on her apron. "But remember what he was—King of France."

Gracie shuddered. To her, he was the ogre who terrorized Europe, the most powerful and most feared man in the world. Yet, in the end, Napoleon had been defeated, and the British had banished him to a place from which he would never escape.

That's how it is for me, she thought. I'll never get away, either.

Right now, she had work to do. While she stayed in the kitchen, she need not set eyes on Napoleon Bonaparte.

A small, frizzled maid called Kitty hopped like a bird between the table and the larder. She cocked her head, watching Gracie. "You're new," she said. "Where you bin?"

"Jamestown."

"You've come all the way from Jamestown!"

"My father's shop doesn't make enough money. I need the work."

"He sells things! Chinese things?"

Gracie didn't tell Kitty that her father came from England. "He sells tobacco and tinned food, and barley and candles... and arsenic for the rats."

"And fireworks?"

"Sometimes he does," snapped Gracie.

"You wouldn't know how to curl lemons."

"Um..."

"I'll have to show you then. You can help out before the washing-up."

Kitty's crinkled fingers deftly shaped lemon strips for decoration on the desserts. "I bin at The Briars since before the

Balcombes," she said. Gracie took this as a warning not to question anything Kitty said.

As soon as dinner was served, Kitty gave a little nod to Mrs. Pratt and said, "Good night." Gracie began to scrub the cooking pots. Water from the boiler scalded her hands. The crude soap stung her skin. Each time a maid went in or out the door, she heard snatches of conversation from the dining room. The heavy, blunt voice in very bad English must be the monster himself. Now and then came a girl's voice in another language.

"Who else is there?" she asked Mrs. Pratt.

"That's Miss Betsy. Betsy Balcombe. She learned to speak French at school in England."

She must be one of the girls Gracie had seen playing on the lawn. She wished she had long fair hair like Betsy, and light skin. Forget the pretty dresses. One day she'd learn to sew like her mother, and make herself a dress. But she couldn't ever change the color of her skin.

IT WAS AFTER ELEVEN O'CLOCK before she scrubbed the sink and stacked the clean dishes on the table.

"You've done well," said Mrs. Pratt. "Mr. George will look after you tomorrow."

Gracie understood that being "looked after" meant being paid.

"I come tomorrow then?"

Mrs. Pratt nodded. "We could use you again. Be here by eight o'clock."

The maids had gone to their quarters and lamps were burning in the Pavilion when Gracie stepped outside, into the darkness.

She stole across the lawn into the shadows of the banyan trees. Shapes mingled eerily, but she was not afraid of the dark or the loneliness of the night. Since her mother died, she'd often been on her own. Stumbling on the uneven track was her only fear.

The night was warm and still, but the air felt cool on Gracie's burning fingers. Holding out her arms for balance, she groped along the rutted path. Now running, now sliding, then stumbling over bumps, she edged down the hill towards Jamestown. As she drew closer, she saw figures moving in the night. Sentries stood on guard at every corner into town, but apart from the soldiers, the streets were deserted. Not another soul could be seen.

Gracie's feet made no sound on the path as she slipped from shadow to shadow. When she came to the street where Hester lived, she began to run. Her dark hair flew out behind her. Her shoes tapped like drumsticks on the cobbles.

"Hey!" called a voice across the road.

Was the soldier calling out to her, Gracie? Could he possibly be someone who knew her? An uncle, perhaps? Or was he just a soldier, questioning a lone figure on the street?

She ran and ran till she reached the door and knew she was safe.

4

"You were awfully late last night," said Hester.

Gracie stared into her bowl of porridge. Weevils like grains of cracked pepper studded the oatmeal, but she was hungry. She gulped down the porridge and helped herself to more from the pot.

"And you had no dinner!" said Alice. "Gracie, you can't go on like this."

"I have to, I've found good work. And..." She was talking through a mouthful of porridge, but she had to eat and she wanted to talk. "And you'll never guess... *he's* there!"

"Who's *he?* And where?"

"At The Briars. Bonaparte!"

"Gracie!" Alice's eyes narrowed. "You didn't go all the way to The Briars?"

"Did you see him?" asked Hester.

Gracie shook her head. "I don't have to see him. That's the good part."

Alice's lips pulled into a thin line. "Have you told your father about this?"

"I haven't spoken to him."

"Then you must. I can't let you go off so far while we're looking after you."

"Plee-ease," said Gracie. "I need to do this. And you don't need to know."

Alice rested both hands on the back of Gracie's chair, and leaned close to her. "Just go and see him. Tell him you're all right."

Gracie nodded, without looking up. "After school, I'll go."

Hester stood her spoon on end and twirled it slowly in the air. "Just think," she said. "You could be talking with an emperor."

"Oh!" Gracie gasped. "I won't ever *talk* to him!"

"Yes," said Alice. "I must say I feel safer with him out of Jamestown."

"He's allowed to walk around," said Gracie.

"But there are guards everywhere, I'm sure."

"Why don't they lock him up?" asked Hester.

In a way, they had, thought Gracie. Here, on St. Helena, he was locked away from the rest of the world. She watched Hester's nose crinkle, till the little clump of freckles almost disappeared. Hester always said she wanted olive skin like Gracie's. She hated her own creamy complexion and the freckles on her nose. In the dry season, the sun burned her an angry red. In the hot and wet, when the sky was gray and the rain fell in torrents, she looked like a pail of milk. She wished she had a drop of Chinese blood in her, too.

Gracie believed Hester said this only to be nice. She pretended to like Gracie for the very reasons some English girls didn't like her. Hester was too kind to upset anyone.

"Are you really going off there again today?" she asked Gracie.

"Of course."

"You *want* to go!"

"No, Hester, I *have* to go."

"And I'll be stuck back here with Mum and Dad."

Gracie didn't think that was a bad place to be. Crammed into a niche in the wall, right beside the kitchen dresser, the Kendrews kept books. Gracie knew the titles of each one, and envied Hester the time to read them. *Robinson Crusoe, Pilgrim's Progress,* and poems and plays by Shakespeare. Alice often told her to take one home, but the shop was not the place for reading. At night, her candle didn't burn brightly enough. To have a free day, reading in the tranquility of the Kendrews' house, was a luxury she dare not dream.

"I bet you wouldn't swap places with me," she told Hester. Especially this afternoon, when she went to see her father.

At least now she could look him in the eye and tell him she had a job. She'd made up her mind. If he showed that he missed her, or needed her, she'd stay.

He looked up when she walked into the shop. "Oh, it's you. Where d'you think you've been?"

"You knew I was safe."

He slammed a drawer shut behind the counter. "How d'you think a father feels when his daughter doesn't come home?"

"I'm sorry."

"Sorry, eh! I'll give you sorry."

"Something happened. Bonaparte came to the boarding house."

"So what does our Gracie do?" He waited for her answer.

"I was angry... and a bit afraid... the stories you'd told me. What might he do to us here?"

"Didn't you think of us! Where's the money going to come from now?" He banged his fists on the counter. Small tins of food bounced in the air and crashed down again.

Gracie jumped in fright, though he'd done it many times before.

"Father, I have work again."

"So now you're coming home?"

Gracie gazed at his pale eyes and at the small hands gripping the counter. "No, I don't think so."

He took a step towards her. "You'll stop here!" he shouted. His cheeks had swollen into blotchy red balloons.

He pointed to the room above the shop. "That's where you belong!"

Gracie barged past him, through the door and up the narrow staircase. "You never listen!" she screamed. "I wish I hadn't come!"

The attic room held no greeting for her. Its once comforting walls enclosed her like a cell, and she couldn't wait to escape. She jerked open the drawer and scooped up her clothes, swept two dresses from hooks and stamped downstairs.

"The Kendrews are nice to me," she cried. "And they want me there."

On her way back through the shop, she saw a handwritten card on a bowl. EGGS 1/– each. A shilling each! Just three days before, they were selling a whole dozen for 3/–. Now there were two thousand extra people on the island who needed to buy food. The soldiers had almost doubled the population. Bonaparte was changing everything, even the price of eggs. How could the paltry few shillings she earned help her father to pay the bills?

It's not my worry, she thought as she flounced out the door. Rose had always told her to take people as she found them. Right now, Father, she said to herself, I don't find you very nice at all.

SHE HAD TIME TO DROP HER CLOTHES into the Kendrews' house before she made her way to The Briars. The guard on the gate looked her up and down and let her pass. As she walked along the path, she saw the gardener sweeping leaves from the crown he'd cut in the grass. When he looked up, his face dissolved into one big smile. He had a mouth like a cavern and teeth like a row of monuments. His skin was darker than hers, and he was much, much older.

"Hello," she said.

The gardener pointed to the Pavilion. "For him," he said. "He talk with me."

"Oh?" He couldn't mean Bonaparte.

"You work?" he asked.

"Yes, in the house."

"Ah, very busy now." His smile warmed her again before he bent back over his broom.

Mrs. Pratt was waiting in the kitchen. "Gracie, good, you're here. We need more water right away."

Kitty flitted across the room and Gracie could feel her eyes inspecting her from top to toe. "You have a clean dress today."

"Most days I do," said Gracie. Not new, but clean.

"And a nice bracelet, too," Kitty pointed to Gracie's wrist.

Gracie covered the bracelet, quickly, with her other hand. "I wore it yesterday,' she said. "I wear it always."

"You wouldn't, if you know what's right for you. Soap and water does them things no good at all."

"Thank you," said Gracie. But she wouldn't be taking the bracelet off for anyone.

This evening, the kitchen had a different air about it. Napoleon's French cook had joined him at the Pavilion and was busy supervising dinner preparations.

"His Majesty likes chicken," he said in halting English.

"His Majesty! Hmph!" said Gracie under her breath.

Most of the time, the cook issued instructions in French. He waved his arms and pointed, and the maids bumped into one another hurrying to please him.

"I bin here a long time," muttered Kitty, "and I never bin bossed around like this."

Gracie did her work and kept out of the way. When she finished the washing-up that night, she wiped her hands on her dress and looked towards Mrs. Pratt.

"See you tomorrow, Gracie," she said.

So she still had a job.

Once again, she began the long walk home. As she took a shortcut across the lawn, a lamp flickered on the path to the Pavilion and she saw a short, stout figure, followed by the lamplighter with a lantern. She turned and ran faster, till she was hidden among the trees.

"Stop there!" called a sentry near the gate.

Gracie kept running. A shot fired in the darkness. She flung herself into a ditch at the side of the road.

Before Napoleon came, the only sounds of the night were

people singing and sometimes a drunken brawl. Nobody chased you with a gun. You could roam the paths of St. Helena and never see a soldier.

One man had changed all that. Because of Bonaparte, everyone's freedom was restricted. Like a hunted animal, Gracie stole down the road to Jamestown. She flitted from shadow to shadow, crouched in gutters and flattened herself under bushes. When she stumbled and fell, she didn't cry out but lay without flinching till it was safe to move again.

The Kendrews' house, at the end of the chase, was not just a home but a haven.

"YOU LOOK AWFUL!" Hester said next morning.

Gracie had to admit, she was worn out.

"Gracie, there's a curfew," explained Alice Kendrew. "Nobody is allowed out at night after nine o'clock. You'll end up in trouble if you go on like this."

Gracie gritted her teeth. "I can sniff out a soldier two hundred paces away. It isn't the guards I'm afraid of. It's him. I get a spooky feeling he's watching me. The lamp goes out in the Pavilion loft, and I know he's at the window."

"So what?" said Hester. "You're no one to him."

Gracie hadn't told Hester of the note she'd written in anger that first day. Yet Napoleon could never know it was she who had written it. Could he?

He was a dark shadow, always threatening. His power was so great that he'd turned island life upside-down, just by being there.

"You're imagining things," said Hester. "You should be more worried about the curfew. Going all that way! What if the soldiers catch you? You could go to jail! And did you ever get paid?"

"Oh, yes, Mr. George gave me seven shillings. There's some for your mother." She reached into her pocket.

Alice waved her away. "Take it to your father, Gracie. Try to make peace with him."

"I don't want to see him," said Gracie.

ALTHOUGH GRACIE'S WORK DIDN'T START UNTIL EIGHT O'CLOCK, she chose to walk to The Briars each afternoon in daylight. Most evenings, she came upon the Malay gardener finishing his day's work near the grape arbor. He was careful to lock the gate into his vegetable garden. Nobody was allowed there without his consent.

This day she found him tending his special patch of lawn. A chair stood beside the crown in the grass.

"Boney sit here," he told Gracie.

She frowned at the chair.

The gardener tapped himself on the chest. "Me, Toby."

"I'm Gracie."

"You still work?"

"Yes, I do."

"Toby work, too. You know Boney?"

She shook her head.

"But Boney know you."

"No!"

"You the girl who cross the grass at night?"

"I *knew* he was watching!"

"He ask me. He no like that."

Gracie shuddered. She was right. There was something sinister about this place. "I'd better go," she said to Toby.

"You be right, miss," he said, and she could feel the hug in his smile.

She had time, so she took a path towards the tinkle of goat bells and cackle of chickens. They were evening sounds she didn't hear in Jamestown. Not far away stood a handsome black stallion. She couldn't take her eyes from his coat, which shone like silver. His ears pricked at the sound of her steps.

"He thinks you might have a carrot," said the groom.

"I haven't got anything."

"Good. Boney doesn't like him to eat between meals."

"He's Bonaparte's horse?"

"He rides him every day."

"You mean, they let him out!"

"Who?"

"Bonaparte."

"Why not? He rides with Captain Poppleton. The guards are everywhere. He'll never get away."

Gracie stroked the horse's head.

"Called Hope, he is."

It was a strange name for a horse, Hope. "No hope," she said, and giggled.

"You got a funny sense of humor. Who are you, anyway?"

Gracie hadn't ever met anyone so blunt.

"Gracie Taverner. I work here now."

"Oh, really!" He raised his head and sniffed. The question-mark lock of hair sprang like a coil across his forehead. "Little Miss Uppity, eh?"

"That's one thing I'm *not,*" she said as she strode away.

After days of walking to work, and late hours, her body felt as lean as a wire stick. The soles of her feet had become as hard as the stones on the island paths. After nights of stealing through the darkness, outwitting soldiers, she could handle a common groom.

She could handle the work, too, the same every day: scalding water, soap gnawing into raw skin, a confusion of voices and many words she didn't understand. She kept her head down over the sink, and went on with her job.

This evening, Mrs. Pratt was waiting. "Ah, there you are, Gracie."

"I'm not late?"

"No, no, but things are going to be different from now on."

So I'm fired again, thought Gracie.

"Mr. George wants to see you. Now."

Gracie's face turned sickly gray. "Wh... where?"

"In his office."

What else have I done wrong? Gracie wondered. So many things. She couldn't think which might get her into the most trouble. She straightened the folds of her dress and ran her fingers through her hair before she walked across the passage to the small office and knocked on the door.

"Yes."

She pushed the door and peered through the opening.

"Well, come in!"

Mr. George left her standing in the center of the room as he rose from his chair behind a desk. "How old are you, child?"

She'd already told him, that first day. "Eleven."

"It seems these late hours are not suitable for someone your age."

"Yes, sir." She was to go.

"So, there has been a request..." He cleared his throat. "*I* request that you work in a different area. Can you come at four o'clock?"

If she hurried, she could get there in time.

"On Saturdays and Sundays, come at noon. The General takes lunch at one."

Gracie felt the blood pulsing at her temples. Her face felt hot. "Thank you, sir, I..."

"Don't thank *me*. You can finish off tonight and start earlier tomorrow. Report to Mrs. Pratt."

How could this have come about? mused Gracie. Good things didn't happen to someone like her.

Until now.

6

It was just like the Kendrews! Every other day they treated her as part of the family, but on Saturdays she became a guest, and first into the bathtub.

William dragged the tin bath beside the hearth and filled it with hot water from the cauldron. In the bedroom, Gracie slipped off her bracelet and placed it on the windowsill. A blink of sunshine captured the stone in its beam and threw a circle of green light around the window. Gracie ran her fingers through the reflection, and found nothing there.

She turned to Hester. "I won't wear my bracelet to work again. I don't want to spoil it."

"But Gracie, you wear it always. You can't leave it here."

Gracie picked it up and pressed it into Hester's palm. "You wear it for me—while I have this job. I know it will be safe with you."

On mornings like this, the island wasn't such a bad place to be. When Gracie set out on the road to The Briars, the town had thrown off its warm, sticky blanket and the clouds had not yet swallowed up the sun. Clean and fresh, she danced along the Saturday road. When she spun on her heels and stretched out her hands, the air felt cool under her arms. Even the goats seemed friendly.

If I owned the day, she thought, I'd keep it like this. I wouldn't let it go.

She shrugged and kept on dancing. Mama would have said, "Don't be selfish, Gracie."

All right, she said to herself. Keep going, Saturday. You don't belong to me.

Nothing belonged to her, except the few shillings she earned from her work. She should take it to her father. One day, she might. But not yet.

She was in for a surprise when she reached The Briars. A huge tent covered part of the lawn, with a connecting walkway to the Pavilion.

"You'll be in the marquee from now on," said Mrs. Pratt. "Come on, I'll show you."

A make-do kitchen had been set up in an annex closest to the Pavilion. In the center of the marquee stood a formal dining table and chairs. The far end of the new shelter had been divided by curtains.

"That's the General's bedroom," whispered Mrs. Pratt.

Through an opening in the curtains, Gracie glimpsed the crown in the grass. Beside it stood a narrow camp bed.

"Am I to make his bed?" asked Gracie.

"Oh, no." Mrs. Pratt looked shocked at the question. "He's brought his own manservant."

Gracie breathed out at last. "It'll be all right, then."

"What's that?"

"Mrs. Pratt, can I ask you something?"

"Of course, child."

"How long is Bonaparte staying here?"

"Till the Longwood house is ready. A few weeks, maybe."

Gracie supposed that after that she'd have to find another job. For the first time, then, it struck her that though Napoleon had cost her the last job, she only had this one because of him.

SOMETHING WAS BOTHERING KITTY. Her face was pinched and tight, with the hint of a storm brewing. She scuttled past Gracie without saying hello, but Gracie heard a mumbling under her breath. "Some people always get their way..."

"Do you need any help, Kitty?"

Kitty spun around. "And what do you think you can do?"

"Anything, if I don't have to see Napoleon."

Kitty pounced on Gracie's words. "We're not to call him Napoleon. He's General Bonaparte now."

"I forgot." Gracie shrugged. "Are names that important?"

"I don't make the rules. I bin here before most, but I don't get any say. See, now you get what you're after—and I'll be here till eleven o'clock."

So that was the trouble! "I didn't ask," said Gracie.

"No? Well, someone fixed it for you!" Kitty flounced away, then came back to face Gracie. "And another thing—don't go talking to that gardener. He's a slave."

"I like him," said Gracie. "And I like his garden, too." She wanted to tell Kitty what she had learned from her mother, that you take people as you find them. And she wanted to say that she was sorry Kitty had been given her late shift. But she didn't.

Instead, she said, "I'll get on with what I have to do, then."

First, she collected fresh water to refill the boilers. As she turned from the well with a bucket in each hand, she saw Toby in the grape arbor with Bonaparte and the younger girl, Betsy. Bonaparte was pointing, and Betsy speaking after him, asking Toby questions.

Gracie was close enough to hear their voices. When Bonaparte turned, for a moment she saw the color of his eyes, now blue, now gray as he watched her.

Bonaparte nodded his head and walked on slowly, parting the leaves to finger the fruit. Toby leaned over and picked a big, purple bunch and handed it to him.

Bonaparte bowed to the slave. "*Merci, mon vieux,*" he said.

"Thank you, my man," interpreted Betsy.

Gracie stood, staring, till the weight of the buckets made her arms ache. Slowly, she traced her way back to the marquee.

If an emperor could talk to a slave, why couldn't she? I'll talk to whomever I like, she decided.

1816

Sometimes Gracie pictured the year like a book. It took a long time to get through, and often she found herself stuck in the hard parts. She worked her way, trying to make sense of it, and when the last page turned it didn't seem like an ending. Life went on just the same.

"You're not going off *again*," said Hester one Sunday morning.

"I have to. I'll be back before dark."

"It's boring here, all by myself. Go on, take me with you?"

"Oh, Hester, I'd like to, but I can't." More than anything, she'd like to have Hester with her on the path to The Briars, but she must make the long walk alone.

Hester pouted. "You have all the luck. I think of you out there, mixing with the Emperor and those people in French dresses and uniforms with gold trimmings, and I think, it isn't fair."

"If only you knew." Gracie held out her hands. "Look, this is what I do. This is what happens to me for a few paltry shillings."

Hester rubbed her fingers, gently, over Gracie's rough palms, then fondled the bracelet on her own wrist. "But when you go back to England, think what you'll have to tell."

"I'll never get to England."

"But I will. And people will ask. What will I tell them? That I saw the Emperor once, and he never came to Jamestown again?"

"Don't talk like that, Hester. I don't want you to go to England."

"I know, but one day we will. One day a ship will come with a letter that says, yes, Dad has a job in Newcastle."

"I suppose I'll have to face it then. Let's walk down to the wharf before I go to work, and I'll tell you things you can talk about, so English people know Bonaparte was really here."

The wind was whisking up the water, clouding the docks in sea mist. Through the film of spray, they saw Peggy Maunder and Jess Brimble walking towards them. The four sat together on the rocks, as they often did, with their backs to the water.

Hester turned and squinted at a bark anchored in the bay. "I don't want to spend weeks on a ship like that. It's so far to anywhere."

"But you *do* want to go to England," said Peggy. "How else are you going to get there?"

"I just want to *be* there. In London there are wide streets and palaces and a huge, enormous cathedral with an aisle so long you can't see the end of it—and sometimes it snows."

"Snow!" Gracie sighed. "I've never seen snow."

"Of course you haven't," said Peggy. "Who has?"

"And you can walk miles and miles through bluebell woods," said Hester. "There are squirrels and robin redbreasts that follow you along the hedgerows."

"Hedgerow?"

"A... a row of hedges all rambled up together."

Jess stared at Hester. "How do you know all this?"

"My mother tells me. Doesn't yours?" She glanced at Gracie and a shadow flicked across her eyes. "I'm sorry. I talk too much."

"It's all right. My mother never lived in a place like that. She couldn't tell me things about England, and Father doesn't want to." Gracie pushed damp hair out of her eyes and turned her face to the sea.

"In Mother's village, there were swans, and houses with thatched roofs," said Peggy. She saw the question in Gracie's eyes. "Sort of reeds, I think, like straw. And there were apples and raspberries..."

"Is there anything bad in England, do you think?"

"No one's told us," said Hester. She began to giggle. "But hey, Gracie was going to tell *me* things. And she has work to do later."

"Wish I could work," murmured Peggy.

"Me, too," said Jess. "With an emperor."

Hester frowned at them. "Gracie doesn't think like that."

"Well, go on, and tell us then," said Jess.

Gracie hadn't expected to be the center of attention. "It's like watching a play out there," she began. "A little French court plonked down in this place. Bonaparte's people treat him as if he's still the greatest man in the world. They call him Your Majesty, and no one talks till he says something. The servants who wait on the tables are dressed in green and silver, and the food! It keeps on coming, soup and chicken and meat and vegetables and the pastry cook makes cakes in the shape of castles. It's like royalty in that marquee."

"Peculiar," said Peggy. "But maybe the English have forgotten about him by now?"

"They'll never forget him," said Gracie. She bit her lip as she remembered the work ahead of her. "I'll tell you what scares me the most. He has all these china plates painted with pictures of himself. Imagine if I broke one in the washing-up!"

"I think he'd eat you!"

Gracie laughed. "I never believed that old story. But it doesn't mean I like him any better."

"Hurry home," said Hester.

Gracie smiled at her friend. More and more, this house felt like home. She wished it was. She felt bad leaving Hester for most of the day.

Hester would have loved to play on the lawn like the Balcombe girls, but she didn't understand that she had to be invited. And that would never happen.

Betsy and her older sister Jane were romping on the grass outside the marquee as Gracie made her way up the avenue of banyan trees.

"Hey, come here!" called a voice.

She turned around.

It was the groom, holding Hope on a rein.

"Are you ordering me around?" she said.

"Yeah?" He grinned. "I wouldn't dare!"

"What, then?"

"I just wanted to say hello."

"Hello, then."

"What's wrong with you? I thought you were someone worth talking to."

Gracie felt a tickle of surprise that anyone should consider her interesting. She'd have to think of something to say now.

"You never told me your name," she said.

"Gilbert Proctor, groom."

"I know that. It's a good job."

"Keeps me happy." He gave Hope a friendly slap on the neck. "But one day I want to ride 'em, not just look after 'em."

"Me, too." The silver-black of the stallion's coat was reflected in her eyes. "I want to ride the goat tracks into the mountains—and one day I want to ride through the streets of London." She didn't know why she said that. It just came to her.

"So who do you think you are!"

She shrugged. "Stupid, that's all."

"Sure."

"Well, then, I have work to do." She just couldn't strike the right note with this boy.

She left him and started along the path by the lawn. The two girls ducked and dodged, while their young brothers ran squealing in circles. The man chasing them was small and broad-shouldered, with dark silky hair spilling over a red handkerchief that covered his eyes. It was Bonaparte.

"*Où êtes-vous?* Where?" he called in a gruff voice.

"*Ici! Ici!* Here!" teased the younger girl, touching his arm and then whipping away again.

"Bet-see!" He swung out both arms and once more, even at this distance, Gracie noticed his small, pale hands. "*Bah, Bet-see! Où es-tu?*"

Gracie stopped, staring. "What's he doing?" she said out loud.

Gilbert was suddenly beside her. "They're playing blind man's bluff."

"Oh, it's you again!" she said. "Won't he hurt them?"

"Why? They do it all the time."

Gracie screwed up her face. "I wouldn't trust him." She put her head down and hurried towards the marquee.

"D'you trust anyone?" he called after her.

"Of course I do!" she snapped. But who? Hester, and Alice and William Kendrew, and after that it was hard to think.

She couldn't help turning back, just once, to steal another look at the game. "Enough!" cried Bonaparte, as he ripped off his blindfold and pointed at Betsy's ankle-length pantaloons. "Bah, pontalons!"

Being poor wasn't all bad, thought Gracie. At least she didn't have to wear things like that.

8

"I SPOKE TO YOUR FATHER YESTERDAY," said Alice.

Gracie waited to hear what Alice had to say.

"The shop's very busy, with all the soldiers in town."

"Business is good, then. So why doesn't he ask me to help?"

Alice clicked her tongue. "He's a stubborn man, your father."

"Well, I'm not going to ask." She couldn't face the effort of trying to get along with a difficult man. She wouldn't go home yet. Unless he asked.

Alice rested her hand on Gracie's shoulder and smiled. "Did I say someone in your family was stubborn!"

While it lasted, Gracie would manage with the job she had now. It gave her no time to play, like the Balcombe girls. But each day, as she trudged up the road to The Briars, she sensed a secret life unfolding before her. She could feel the pull of this different world, drawing her into it.

No matter how hard she tried to dodge running into Bonaparte, she came upon him everywhere she went. When she walked through the garden, he was there, strolling with his hands behind his back. When she took a longer route past the orange grove, he was sitting under the trees, dictating to his aide.

There he was scuffling on the lawn with the Balcombe girls. "Bah!" he said, and sank into a chair. When he took off his hat, she saw the band of sweat sticking his hair to his forehead. He looked tired and a little bit sad, but he smiled at the smaller Balcombe boy and let him crawl across his knees. The boy delved into Bonaparte's pockets and fished out something that might be licorice. He popped it into his mouth and pulled a face.

"*C'est bon, n'est-ce pas?* Good, eh?" said Bonaparte.

The boy spat out the licorice.

"It makes your teeth black," said Betsy.

"*Tu es une insolente!*"

"I'm not rude," she said. "It's true, *c'est vrai*—licorice makes your teeth black."

Bonaparte shook his head, and let the boy down from his lap. "*Tu ne seras jamais soldat… jamais!*" he said. "You—never a soldier!" The boy didn't seem to care, or maybe he didn't understand.

When Bonaparte turned and saw Gracie, she held her hand to her face and hurried on.

ONE SATURDAY MORNING, she left Jamestown early after bath time and hiked up the interweaving goat tracks into the mountains behind The Briars. The sun was already simmering above the peak when she heard voices behind a wall of rocks.

She stopped and listened, and recognized the broken English of the man she spent her days trying to avoid. In a moment she saw the cock of his hat as he and his party of three women crossed onto her path.

Gracie edged into the rough at the side of the narrow track. At the same time, a group of African slaves straggled up the path from another direction. Each carried a heavy sack on his shoulders. Their bare chests shone with sweat, and Gracie heard the strain of their breathing as they came closer.

"Move out of the way!" called one of the women. "Napoleon is here!"

Bonaparte raised his arm to beckon the slaves on.

"*Madame,*" he said. "*Ils sont lourdement chargés.* Heavy loads, indeed."

Gracie pressed herself against a rock till the slaves had passed, and Bonaparte and his party continued on their way.

Then she turned and went back the way she had come.

LATE THAT AFTERNOON, as the great hulk of the mountain shrouded The Briars in shadow, Gracie saw a short, plump figure slot a key in the gate and let himself into the walled vegetable garden.

Was this Bonaparte also a thief? She watched with her mouth hanging open as he walked straight to the banana palm. He stretched to pick one from the bunch, stripped back the peel and gulped down the fruit as if he hadn't eaten all day.

Ripe pomegranates hung nearby, and before he left he picked three or four. He locked the gate behind him, and slipped the key into his pocket.

Each morning, Toby searched his garden for footprints, expecting to find children had stolen his fruit and vegetables. What would he do when he recognized the boots of Bonaparte?

I won't tell anyone, Gracie decided. It's not my problem. But she couldn't help wondering where Bonaparte had found the key.

"Hi there!" called someone behind her. "You still speaking to me?"

She'd know that voice anywhere. "Hello, Gilbert." Had he, too, seen Bonaparte in the vegetable garden?

"Don't look so worried," he said. "It spoils your good looks. Come and say hello to the horses."

Hope hung his head over the stable door and pricked his ears as she came near.

"See, he knows you," said Gilbert. "He's one happy horse."

Gracie knew again the flush of warmth she'd felt at his words once before. She must think of something to say to Gilbert. "Do you live at The Briars?" she asked.

"Just outside... over there." He gestured with his head. "Dad runs the carriages for the Balcombes. I've never lived anywhere else."

"Me neither. I mean, Jamestown."

"It's a long walk, coming here every day."

She nodded. "I'll survive."

"*C'est bon.*"

"Eh?"

"That's good. I've learned some French from Boney."

"Why?"

"Why not? He tries to talk English."

Gracie leaned her cheek against the horse's neck. "I haven't spoken a word to him."

"But he's noticed you."

"No!"

"Boney gets to know everyone. He and Toby have long talks, and neither of them understands a word."

When he laughed, his eyes disappeared and his crinkly hair danced as if it were on springs.

"I talk to Toby, too," said Gracie.

"I bet he hasn't given you a key to his precious garden. Only Bonaparte has one of those."

So Bonaparte wasn't a thief!

"Toby trusts him," said Gilbert. "Word's getting around that Boney wants to buy Toby, and set him free."

"So what's going to happen?"

"Toby says no. It's too long since he was brought here as a slave. He doesn't know anything else now. It's said he had a daughter back in Malaya, about the same age as Miss Betsy is now, when he was taken away. But he doesn't speak of his family. He's all alone, but he's happy the way he is."

If someone was happy being a slave, could you be happy as a prisoner? Gracie wondered. Could Bonaparte ever be content living on St. Helena? No, not when he considered what he had been and what he was now. Not when he'd left behind an empire and his small son. She still had her father, and her father had her, even if they weren't speaking. There was some kind of thread linking a father with his child. She felt herself teetering again on the thin line between love and hate.

Gilbert leaned towards her. "Wake up, there! I want to let you into a secret, about something you once said. One day, I want to go to London, too."

"I'll never get there."

"Don't say that. Save up, like I am, and you never know."

Gracie glanced about her, at the darkness that had enclosed

them without her noticing. "I know one thing," she said. "I should have been on the road home before this."

"One day, I'll take you in a carriage," he called after her.

"Be serious," she said.

9

SOMETHING WAS KEEPING GRACIE AWAKE AT NIGHT.
She couldn't get Bonaparte out of her head. All the fear and
hatred she'd felt before he came was mixed up with what she'd
seen of him at The Briars.

Now, she didn't know what to think. She wished he'd never
come to the island. She wished she'd never heard of him.
Yet life for her was no worse than it had been before he arrived. What has he done to me, she thought, that I should
hate him so? All she'd seen was an ordinary man who treated
people decently, even with respect. People like her.

Someone had stepped in to give her better working hours,
and she couldn't help wondering...

At times like this, Gracie felt her mother looking over her
shoulder. She slipped back the blanket and lit a candle, so she
could see to write.

HESTER STIRRED IN HER BED. "What are you doing?"

Gracie dropped the pen and covered the paper with her hand. "Nothing."

"But you are! Who are you writing to?"

Gracie blushed. "No one."

It was almost true. She wouldn't be sending the letter.

Dear Bonaparte, she had written,

> *Do you know it was me who wrote that note the first day?*
> *Is this why I can't ever get away from you now?*
> *Sometimes, I'm sorry.*
> *Gracie.*

She blotted the ink, folded the page and stowed it in a small box with her belongings. She could never speak to Bonaparte, to ask him face to face. But it made things easier, getting it off her chest. Already, she felt lighter inside.

Hester sat up in bed, with her hands clasped over her knees. "How much longer is Bonaparte staying at The Briars?" she asked, as if she'd been reading over Gracie's shoulder.

"They haven't said, but I've heard that the Longwood house is nearly ready."

"What then?"

Gracie didn't want to think. The job at The Briars would be finished, and Longwood was over an hour's walk from there, at Deadwood Plain. The long walk was out of the question. "I suppose I'll have to find something in Jamestown."

"Go and see your father."

Gracie shook her head, wildly, furiously, like a puppy after a bath.

In the candlelight, Hester fixed her gaze on her friend. "Gracie, I want you to."

"Why, what's wrong?"

Hester's face was so pale that the freckles stood out on her nose.

Gracie grabbed her, pinning her to the bed. "Tell me! What's happened?"

"Mum wouldn't tell you yet. A ship came in today. There was a letter."

Gracie slumped onto the bed. "So you're going. When?"

"The ship's having repairs." Hester spoke in a whisper, as if she didn't want to say. And Gracie didn't want to hear. Yet she couldn't stop herself from asking. "Tell me when!"

"Maybe Saturday."

"Saturday! That's only five days!"

Hester shrugged. "It could be Sunday."

"Don't tell me any more."

"But Gracie, we'll always be friends, always keep in touch. And one day..."

"One day what?"

Hester crinkled her nose, making the freckles disappear. "One day I might see you in England."

If only Gracie could believe it.

"But now, you see, you must go back to your father."

How could Gracie even think about that? First, she needed to believe that Hester was leaving. She'd be alone.

"I suppose you could stay with the Maunders up the street. Peggy's your friend—and what about the Brimbles?"

"Mmm."

"Why don't you ask?"

"Hester, I'm not a beggar. Something will turn up." Already she was thinking that if she became a domestic servant, she'd have a bed to sleep in and a roof over her head. But she'd miss school, and she still had lots to learn.

There was plenty of work in Jamestown now; more work than people to fill the jobs. But most of all, she needed somewhere to live.

She flung herself flat on the bed and hid her face in the pillow. If only she could sweep all this from her mind. If she could wake up in the morning, and find that nothing had changed.

It was no use fooling herself. Already, Alice was clearing out cupboards and packing things in boxes.

William Kendrew came home early from the dock next evening and started mending leaking slates and fixing a window that wouldn't shut. "The navy's taking over the house," he said.

He turned to Gracie. "Now, what about you?"

"I'll be all right." Her voice came out as if she were far away, adrift and alone.

William put his hand on her shoulder. "Don't worry, Gracie, I'll go and see your father tomorrow."

"Don't you dare!" she cried. "He'll only get mad at you." Samuel expected Gracie to crawl back. Well, she wasn't crawling to anyone.

"Let's not spoil our last few days together," said Alice.

Gracie tried to smile, but her mind wouldn't stop spinning. She'd saved more than five guineas during the time she'd been at The Briars. Alice and William Kendrew had refused to take a penny of it. At least she'd be able to pay for a bed, some-where, for a night or two.

In the meantime, her work at The Briars continued. The sentry at the gate nodded to her each day, as if she were part of the property. She knew the routine of Bonaparte's court, and what needed doing in the marquee. There was water to be collected, boilers checked, chickens to be plucked, potatoes peeled, pots and dishes washed, dried and carried to shelves in the Pavilion.

She peered at Kitty as she worked beside her at the big table. "Thank you for teaching me how to do this." She could now manage a perfect twist of lemon.

Kitty gave a grudging nod. "I bin doing it a long time."

When next she saw Toby, she waved across the garden. Toby put down his wheelbarrow and sent a smile she could feel as she ran towards him.

"Toby!" she called, and wondered why she couldn't wait to talk with him. "Toby, are you busy?"

"Not too busy, miss."

"How's Bonaparte?" She wasn't sure why she asked.

"Boney be going soon. I miss him. I miss you."

"Oh, Toby, when?"

"A few days, they tell me Sunday."

"It's all ending. And I have to find somewhere else to live, too." She shouldn't be telling him this. But Toby had deep, comforting eyes that made her want to confide in him.

His old face collapsed like a bag full of creases. "This no good. Where your mama, your papa?"

"My father's busy in his shop. He doesn't have time for me."

Toby leaned on his spade. "Not true. Something very wrong."

Gracie hung her head. "I didn't mean to tell you, Toby. I'll be all right, but what about you?"

"I stay, miss. Good place, this." Toby was contented, not wanting anything more.

In a way, she was happy here, too. "I won't say goodbye yet," she said. "We have a few more days."

Toby stooped over his barrow and watched as she walked away.

10

EVERYONE WAS MOVING. Gracie felt the bustle of change all about her.

The Kendrews turned their house upside-down. Cupboards were emptied and floors stacked with trunks and crates and cases.

"It's sailing Monday," said William, when he came home from work. "Three more days." He sat on a sealed crate and sighed. "Who'd have thought this day would ever come?"

He grabbed his daughter's hand as she passed. "Take in everything about the island these last few days, Hester, because we'll never be back."

Gracie sat among the clutter at the kitchen table, eating the stew Alice had saved for her. Already locals were coming with farewell gifts. Alice left the door open to the street, so friends didn't have to knock. A lantern burned in the doorway.

Yet this time, there was a knock. "Come in, if you've had a bath this week," called William.

"It's me, Samuel."

Gracie put down her knife and fork, and listened.

"Well, come on in," said William.

It was unlike Samuel to wait until invited. Gracie pushed back her chair and stood to face him.

He shuffled uneasily, trying to smile but not directing his gaze at anyone in the room. His clothes were neater than usual at the end of the day, and Gracie guessed he'd changed into clean trousers and jacket.

"How are you, Samuel?" asked Alice.

Hester glanced towards Gracie and went to stand beside her.

"I don't want to intrude," said Samuel. "But I need to see Gracie."

"Sit down. How can we help?"

Samuel didn't sit down. He looked across the table at his daughter. "Gracie, I'll understand if you don't want to see me..."

She didn't answer.

"... but I'm going to ask a favor."

Gracie gripped the table and waited.

"Would you... could you come home?"

"Why?" Her voice was quiet and calm.

"Because... because I'm lonely and because I need help in the shop."

It must have hurt him to admit that he needed her. He was being honest.

Gracie hesitated, but only for a moment. "All right," she said. "I'll come." She'd be honest, too. "I need a place to live."

Samuel took a step towards her, and stopped. He'd aged in the few weeks since she'd seen him. She noticed new creases under his eyes, and a grayness on his cheeks. His lip trembled.

Gracie looked away.

"I'll come, Father. Tomorrow, after I've finished at The Briars, I'll come."

She sensed the sigh that soughed through the room, as if a breeze had blown away some of the cares of the world.

II

IT WAS HER LAST DAY AT THE BRIARS. She'd go early to say goodbye to Mrs. Pratt and Toby and Gilbert, and to Kitty, too. No doubt Bonaparte would cross her path again, somewhere, during the day. Only once—yesterday—had she failed to come upon him somewhere on the estate. Well, she wouldn't be saying goodbye to him, because she hadn't ever said hello.

Now that he was going farther away, she could put him out of her life.

First, she went to the stables. "I hoped you'd come," said Gilbert. "I want to show you the new horses. The Admiral sent them from Jamestown for Boney and his people to ride to Longwood."

Gracie raced the length of the stables, peering into each stall. Gilbert watched her and laughed. "They'll be gone in the morning."

"And then, what do you do?"

"What I've always done. It won't be the same, though, after all this."

All this had changed so many things.

"And you won't be here any more," he said.

She nodded. "I'm going to help my father."

"I might see you in Jamestown, then."

"Would you come on a horse?"

"Not me. They don't belong to me."

"No carriage!" She clicked her tongue, teasing. "And not even a horse!"

"Just you wait!"

NEXT THERE WAS TOBY. She sought him out in the vegetable garden, but found him tending his roses. He held one out to her as she came near.

Gracie's cheeks flushed. No one had ever given her a flower, especially not a rose like this one, a loose cup of yellow ruffles with a musky scent she could smell without dipping her nose into its petals.

"I miss you," said Toby. "You come again."

"Oh, I'll try."

His dark eyes searched her face. "You all right, miss? You have nice house now?"

"I'm all right, Toby. I'm with my father."

Toby's face opened into a smile. "I much better, then." He went on picking roses. "These for Boney," he said.

Gracie followed him along the path. "Toby, tell me something. Does... did Bonaparte know me, do you think?"

"Boney, he know everyone." His puzzled smile made her feel she'd asked a silly question. So that was his answer?

Toby shook his head, but he wasn't thinking of her now. "Boney know roses," he said. "Many, many roses. But tomorrow, none. Nothing. No roses at Longwood, not one thing. Everything gone on Deadwood Plain."

"I've never been that far," said Gracie. "But one day I might. Bonaparte will be all right there, won't he?"

Toby leaned close to her, and looked around before he spoke. "I little bit worried," he said.

MRS. PRATT BUSTLED INTO THE MARQUEE and called Gracie to the kitchen in the main house. "Today, the General is lunching with the family." She wrapped her arms around her cushiony middle. "He doesn't want to leave, you know."

Gracie wasn't surprised. Longwood sounded a horrible place.

"From tomorrow, we'll be back to the old days. But we'll never forget these weeks. You won't, either."

Gracie supposed she was right. "Thank you for looking after me," she said.

"You've been a help, child. Take care, now."

Even Kitty looked on Gracie kindly today. "You bin no trouble," she said. All the same, she seemed relieved that life would soon be back to normal.

While lunch was being served, Gracie heard scraps of talk from the dining room, a constant chatter of English, Betsy's precise French and the unmistakable, harsh voice of Bonaparte.

"*Je t'en prie de me rendre visite.*"

"*Oui, oui.* Father, we *will* visit Boney at Longwood, won't we?"

"Of course."

"*J'y vais, le coeur gros.*"

"Father, Boney says he goes with a heavy heart."

"I understand."

Then Bonaparte was speaking in English. "I go to a place not so nice as this. *Les murs sont moisis et on y trouve les rats.*"

"Ugh! Moldy walls! But we all have rats," said Betsy.

It could have been any family meal, if you didn't know who was there.

When Gracie left The Briars for the last time, she still hadn't spoken a word to Bonaparte.

HESTER AND GRACIE MOVED ABOUT THE HOUSE without speaking. Gracie wanted to say, It isn't that I don't want to talk to you. It's just that I can't. Words wouldn't come. Deep down, she knew Hester felt the same.

Gracie was going back to her father. And on Monday, the Kendrews would be gone.

Hester stood close to Gracie. "It's time for you to take this back." She slipped the jade bracelet from her wrist and over Gracie's fingers.

Gracie wanted to say, You keep it. But she couldn't, for her mother's sake as much as her own. "Thank you for keeping it safe," she said.

She had nothing to give Hester, nothing special here or back at the shop that a girl of nearly twelve would want to take as a keepsake to England. Gracie owned no necklaces or rings; no trinkets or knickknacks decorated her room. Every book she'd read had been a schoolbook or borrowed from the Kendrews.

She'd think of something. She still had a day and a bit, and she wasn't seeing very clearly today.

Already, the house was almost as empty as she felt inside. Furniture and trunks stood stacked at the door, ready for carts to take them to the wharf.

It was time for Gracie to leave. Alice Kendrew helped to pack her few belongings in a case.

"It's not goodbye yet, Gracie," she said. "There's plenty of time tomorrow."

It would be Sunday. "Yes, I'll come then, to say goodbye to Mr. Kendrew."

"But you'll be at the quay on Monday?" said Hester.

Gracie stared at the bare floorboards. "If the shop's busy, I don't know whether Father will let me off." She picked up the suitcase and remembered to thank Alice for having her, before she blundered out of the house.

"Ah, Gracie!" Samuel opened the door to her. "You look tired. I've cooked a good dinner for us tonight."

Her father wasn't much of a cook. She knew he'd made a special effort. Gracie could smell vegetables cooking, and some sort of beef. They didn't often have meat, and if he cooked it long enough it wouldn't be too tough.

"Put your things in your room, Gracie, and then I'll show you what's what in the shop." His eyes held a glint of good news and a promise of peace.

When she came back to the front of the shop, she held out her hand to Samuel. "Father, I've saved five guineas. Here..."

"No, Gracie, it's yours. The shop's doing well. You keep it."

For the first time, Gracie looked around the walls. The

shelves were stacked full, and the floor was lined with sacks of flour, sugar, rice, dried beans and candied fruit.

Samuel stood back, waiting for her reaction.

"It's so different!"

"Business has never been better," he said. "You won't be bored in the shop now."

Gracie walked up and down, inspecting the goods.

"We'll bag up some orders tomorrow," said Samuel.

While he served dinner, Gracie unpacked her clothes and found Alice Kendrew had slipped in a slim volume of poetry titled *Stars and Primroses*. Alice knew they were Gracie's favorite poems.

The pages spilled over with primroses and snowdrops, oxlips and bluebells, with frost and snow and scatterings of autumn leaves, all things Gracie had never seen. In England soon, primroses would be peeping through the hedgerows. Here, except in places like The Briars, nothing grew but cactus and ordinary old geraniums.

Gracie lay in bed that night and read the poem she liked most, *Hide not your face, pale primrose...*

Before her candle burned out, she pushed back the blanket and sat at the small table that doubled as dressing table and desk. On a sheet of paper, she wrote in a clear hand:

I, *Grace Rosita Taverner, aged 11 years and 10 months, of Jamestown, St. Helena, solemnly vow and declare that I shall meet Hester Kendrew on the island of England before I am grown up.*

SIGNED: *Grace Taverner*

"Would English primroses grow here?" she asked Samuel next morning.

"No chance," he replied. "Why do you ask?"

"I thought we could have a garden."

Samuel stroked his chin. Following his normal Sunday habit, he hadn't shaved. A gray stubble shadowed his cheeks. "Gracie, we haven't the time to struggle with gardens. This is a harsh place."

"Couldn't we try?"

He took a long, deep breath, and Gracie felt she'd tested him too far. She waited for an outburst, but no words came; only a hopeless, heavy sigh.

"It's all right," she said quickly. "I was only thinking."

It was no use, thinking. Nobody she knew in Jamestown had a garden. Where could they plant something? All about them was sea and rock. The front of Samuel's shop opened straight onto the street. The walled backyard, which held only the privy and a line to hang out the washing, was solid rock. There was no room, and no soil for any plant to grow there. Gracie knew that if she sat potted plants on the window ledge, the wind would lift them and blow them away.

"Other things might grow here," Samuel said suddenly. "I'll look into it."

Parents always said they'd look into it when they hoped you'd forget about something. Then they'd change the subject, which was just what Samuel did.

"We'll get those orders packed today, so you can go to school tomorrow. Later, I thought we might take a walk along the waterfront, see the vessels out there, watch the guards change over at noon, and then say our goodbyes to the Kendrews."

Gracie nodded. "Would you like me to clean up the shop first?"

They were being too polite to each other, and they both knew it.

"No, no, today's a rest day."

Nevertheless, it took almost half the morning weighing out and bagging and labeling Monday's orders.

Samuel put one bag aside.

"Who's it for?" asked Gracie. "It hasn't got a name."

"Pierre will collect it," he said.

Pierre. She didn't know any Pierre. She peered into the bag: candied oranges and raisins and licorice.

"It's all right," said Samuel. "I'll know when he comes. Now let's get going, before the wind blows up."

Together, they stepped into the bustle of Jamestown.

"There are so many soldiers," said Gracie.

"Not as many now, since they started moving up to Deadwood Plain."

It seemed to Gracie that soldiers still outnumbered residents. They walked in twos and threes, criss-crossing the street, calling out to one another.

She studied the face of each one who passed, searching for a likeness to her father. Did Samuel flinch at the sight of the tall, uniformed figure with the enquiring glance? Gracie couldn't tell. Samuel brushed past the soldiers with his gaze fixed on the road.

Gracie longed to ask him, "Father, what happened to Uncle Isaac?" In her mind, he'd become Uncle Isaac, though to Samuel it was as if he'd never existed. The question was on the tip of her tongue, yet she couldn't ask.

"So many ships," she said, instead.

Small boats sailed close to shore. In the outer harbor, single-masted sloops of war lay at anchor beside barks and brigantines. Gracie wondered which ship would leave for England next afternoon.

When they reached the Kendrews' house and Samuel knocked on the door, she heard a hollow echo. That's the way I feel inside, thought Gracie. Last words were so important that nobody could think what to say. Nobody behaved like themselves that morning.

Gracie wanted to run away, to chop today out of the calendar. The Kendrews' house had always been a place of comfort. How could she remember her friends like this, in a stiff, near empty room? It was as if the warmth they wanted to share had gone before the ship sailed.

They stood on the bare boards and looked at one another. "It's good of you to come," said William.

"How could we not?" cried Gracie. "One last time!"

Alice put an arm around Gracie's shoulder and held her close.

"Gracie and I owe you a lot," said Samuel, in a voice that wasn't his own.

"Nonsense," said William. "Don't talk like that!" He tapped the wooden trunk that held their most valuable possessions. "We could sit down here."

Samuel shook his head. "We only called to say goodbye."

"Thank you for coming," said William as they went to leave. He couldn't think of a joke to crack today.

And Gracie couldn't bring herself to say goodbye. She held out a small envelope to Hester. "This is all I have."

"What is it?" asked Hester.

"It's a promise."

13

IT WAS AS IF SHE'D NEVER BEEN AWAY FROM HOME.

When Gracie came back from school on Monday, she slipped straight behind the counter. Almost all the new customers were soldiers and sailors. Gracie noticed that Samuel left her to serve the soldiers.

More and more, a feeling grew inside her that he was shying away from something, that one day his brother might walk into the shop. With Gracie here, it would be easier for Samuel to avoid a meeting. Was that why he needed her back in the shop?

"Who's next?" she asked.

A young soldier stepped forward and pointed to the middle shelf. "Tobacco, please."

Being busy kept Gracie's mind from the hour the Kendrews' ship was to sail. Well, almost. She was aware that the day was drifting away, and soon the Kendrews would be done.

Samuel walked to the door and peered along the street.

"Gracie," he said. "Why don't you go down to the wharf? Say goodbye to your friends."

"Are you sure we're not too busy here?"

Samuel tapped her on the shoulder. "Go on... go!"

Gracie grabbed a shawl and flung it around her shoulders. A warm wind whipped up the road from the sea, and the charcoal sky warned of a storm coming.

A handful of neighbors huddled by the quay. Gracie began to run as she saw a small boat pulling away from shore. William and Alice Kendrew crouched on either side of their big wooden trunk. Hester sat at the stern, looking back. She peered across the widening stretch of sea, then raised her arm and waved.

Gracie waved back.

"I'll write," called Hester. Her words were whisked away on the wind.

"I'll write," echoed Gracie. Sixty-seven days to get there, she thought, and another sixty-seven before the letter comes back. I'll write and write, she promised.

The small boat tossed on the slate-gray water. It drew alongside the ship, and sat smacking against the hull while the Kendrews climbed, one by one, up a ladder to the deck. Hester's light dress billowed about her, waving, waving in the wind.

Gracie could just make out their figures, standing facing the shore before the wind grew fiercer and rain slashed into her face, blotting the ship from view. But she heard the boards creak and clank as sails were hoisted and the ship shuddered into an open sea.

1817

14

GRACIE FELT ABANDONED. Hester had gone. Work that
took her outside Jamestown was finished. She spent her days
stepping around her father, anxious not to rouse his temper. It
was as if she were walking on tiptoes, speaking in a whisper,
trying to smooth a rough sea.

She suspected she was growing more like her mother. Not
just her eyes, her hair and her skin, but in the way she han-
dled her father. She was learning how to calm him; or perhaps,
how to keep calm herself.

There were good things about being home. The calluses
on her feet had healed, and her fingers no longer burned and
itched. Bonaparte was far away, out of sight at last, and almost
gone from her thoughts.

Almost. The power he'd held over the world, and his court
at The Briars, lingered in her mind and she knew he'd taken
some hold on her life, too.

Every day except Sunday, the man called Pierre arrived on

horseback for his order. And every time, he hardly spoke, just paid his money and said, "Same, next day."

Most days he came when Gracie was at school. But sometimes it was late afternoon, when she was there to serve him.

She took her time collecting his order, trying to think of ways to keep him in the shop. But Pierre was always in a hurry, as if he had a job to do. He touched his cap and left without saying goodbye.

"Who is this Pierre?" she asked Samuel. And why did he come every day, for the same things?

"He comes from out of town," said Samuel. And, as he always did, he changed the subject. "Which reminds me, Gracie, I forgot to tell you that a young man called to see you yesterday."

She didn't know any young men.

"On a horse."

"A horse! Was it Gilbert Proctor?"

"He didn't say. He looked pretty pleased with himself till I told him you were at school."

It had to be Gilbert. He'd been allowed to ride one of the horses—and she'd missed seeing him! Perhaps he'd come again some day.

"Is he a friend of Hester's?" asked Samuel.

"No!" snapped Gracie. "He's a friend of mine." Yet she couldn't blame her father for expecting her not to have friends. "When do you think I'll hear from Hester?" she asked.

Samuel gazed at the ceiling, as if it held a calendar or a map of the world. "With a ship every four months, who can tell? But soon, perhaps soon."

"Will it be snowing in England?"

He smiled. "Not likely, but cold. And soon it will be spring."

The primroses would show their faces, thought Gracie. Her father hadn't ever spoken of England like this. Gracie wanted to know more. "And will they see the guards outside the Palace?"

His eyes clouded. "How would I know?"

"I only wondered," said Gracie. "You must have seen them, often."

"Yes, enough." And then he changed the subject. He leaned towards her, and his voice was soft. "You know, Gracie, whatever you want to be, I'll let you be. I won't ruin your life by saying you must be a nursemaid or a seamstress or a wife."

Gracie decided to store this in her mind, and one day she'd have the courage to ask whether it included *where* she wanted to be.

IT WAS LATE ON A SATURDAY when Gilbert came again. He hitched his horse to a rail and sauntered into the shop.

"That's him!" said Samuel. "The boy who came before."

Before Gilbert could speak, Gracie touched him on the arm and led him outside.

"What's up?" he asked.

"I'm not sure what Father will think."

"He seems a nice enough old boy to me."

She looked at Gilbert's polished boots and spotless gray jacket. "I'm pleased you came."

"I had to come to town," he said.

"Oh, is that all?"

"So I thought I'd come and tell you, Toby asks about you."

"How is he?"

"As busy as ever. Once a week, he gives me all this stuff to take out to Longwood—fruit and flowers for Bonaparte."

Gracie felt a stirring of interest in the place she'd never seen.

"Is it really awful?"

"Not that bad, and not so nice, either. It's a dead place. There's not a scrap of garden, only one tree. Boney wanders about and doesn't know what to do with himself."

How Bonaparte must hate it, thought Gracie. She was going to ask Gilbert about the Balcombes when another horseman trotted into the street and stopped outside the shop. Pierre dismounted and smiled at Gracie as he tethered his horse. He nodded to Gilbert.

"You know him?" asked Gracie.

"He's Boney's aide."

"Why?" she murmured.

Gilbert peered at her. "Because he came from France with him."

"No, I mean why would he come here every day?"

Gilbert shrugged. "Search me. To keep Boney happy, I suppose."

But *why?* The shock of discovering that the mysterious Pierre came from Bonaparte blew all other thoughts from Gracie's mind. She couldn't think of anything else to say.

He stared at her leaden face. "Okay, then, have you anything to say to Toby?"

"Yes, tell him to be happy. And tell him... tell him one day I'll have a garden as good as his."

"Then that will be in another country," said Gilbert.

Perhaps, she thought. And *if only.* She wanted to add, Tell Toby I'll come to visit him, but she didn't know when. Her mind was churning. Once again, Bonaparte had intruded on her life, and she couldn't think clearly at all. She didn't want Gilbert to leave, but couldn't think of anything more to say to him.

"See you sometime, then," called Gilbert as he rode away.

GRACIE STUMBLED BACK INTO THE SHOP. It was almost closing time, and the customers had left.

"Father!" she cried, with her jaw set firmly, just like his. "Father, why didn't you tell me Pierre came from Bonaparte?"

Samuel held up his hands. "What difference does it make?"

"It's just... peculiar. Why? Why does he come?"

Samuel shut the door of the shop and flopped on a stool behind the counter. "He comes from Bonaparte," he said softly.

"I *know* that! *Why?*"

"Bonaparte came here himself," said Samuel.

"He came here!"

Samuel patted the stool beside him. "Come and sit down, Gracie." He cupped his hand over hers. "Before they moved to Longwood, he came with Captain Poppleton. I didn't recognize him at first. He was dressed like a worker, in baggy breeches and a sackcloth jacket, and a sunhat covered most of his face."

Gracie stared at her father as he went on talking. "He was so gentle, but there was a power in his eyes."

"So what did he want?"

"He wanted you to be looked after."

The words jolted through Gracie like an electric current. "Me?" she stuttered. "He doesn't even know me." Yet Toby had said he *did* know her. And somehow, she'd suspected it all along. She felt he'd been watching, and though she wouldn't admit it, even to herself, he'd been behind something that happened to her.

"He didn't like everything he saw at The Briars," said Samuel. "Children should be at home, with their parents, he said."

"So...?"

"He asked me to have you back here, where you belong."

Gracie gazed at her hands, twisting in her lap. "You had to be asked, then."

"I wanted you here all along."

"He bribed you!" She leaped off the stool, glaring at him. "How dare he! How dare *you*! You didn't want me here at all—till someone offered you money!" Her voice grew hoarser. "*He bribed you!*"

"No, Gracie. He made me swallow my pride."

At the sight of him then, Gracie swallowed her words, but not her rage. She stood, staring, her shoulders heaving. How could she live here, knowing this?

Samuel's face was ashen. He'd shrunk, not just in her eyes, but really. "I know it looks bad, Gracie. I... I've never been any good at saying what I feel."

Gracie breathed deeply, trying to understand. Her own father was being paid to keep her. What did Bonaparte think she was, just a piece of furniture or a tin trunk to be delivered to the door? "So Pierre comes every day, and helps pay to keep me."

"Gracie, Bonaparte wasn't the reason I asked you back. He gave me the strength to do it."

Gracie sat back on the stool beside her father and gazed over his head to the wall. She heard his voice as if it came from another room. "I told Bonaparte, no, he mustn't do it, but he offered, just to be a customer with an order every day. He insisted, and he's kept his word."

"And how long will this go on, then?"

Samuel shrugged. "As long as Bonaparte lives—twenty or thirty years. You don't need to worry about that now."

Gracie didn't want to think of another twenty or thirty years in this place. When she stood up, her legs were shaking.

"Gracie," said Samuel. "Don't be like that. I wanted you back here, more than anything." His shoulders sagged. Gracie didn't want to pity her father, but she felt more sorrow than anger as the thin line between love and hate shriveled and blurred inside her. She felt herself pulled one way and then the other.

Couldn't he see that a man shouldn't be paid for being a father? A few months, even weeks ago, she'd have flown off the handle and walked out on him. Perhaps she'd grown up, for she could see no sense in turning her back on him. Samuel was a humble man who had done the right thing for the wrong reason. He'd been talked into it by an emperor who had become a man.

16

Dear Hester,

Your letter came today. I badly needed to hear from you. Who else can I talk to? Sometimes I don't know what to think. I'm not sure that Father wants me after all, and even though I'm far from Bonaparte now, I can't free myself from him. One man I know well—and don't. The other I don't know at all. And yet there is something I don't understand and can't explain.

You've been gone so long. I still don't look at your place when I pass. I wish I could see your English house, with the stream at the back and bluebells in the woods.

And guess what? Some time ago, I asked Father about primroses, and he said they wouldn't grow here, but something else might. Our latest order came on the ship with your letter— crates of canned food and things—and two packets of everlasting seeds! Sometimes he takes no notice of me and then I find he's been listening. So perhaps he does care a bit.

Wouldn't you like to see everlastings blooming on St.

Helena! For Father's sake, I had to plant the seeds, but when I went outside I knew it was hopeless. Where, here, could I have a bed of everlastings? A bed of anything? Still, I had to try. The Maunders grew geraniums, so I borrowed a trowel and tried to dig some soil from around the clothesline. You know, like I do, there isn't any. I hit hard rock and nearly broke the trowel. In the end, I asked Father what to do. He gave me a bag of stuff called "earth mix" from Africa and I filled an old wooden cask with it and set it against the privy wall so it wouldn't blow away. I planted half a packet of seeds, and I'll let you know what happens.

All the other letters I've written are waiting to go with this one. Will you have time to read them?

And one more thing, please don't tell me too much about the village pony club. It only makes me feel jealous.

Love, Gracie

When she'd blotted the ink and sealed the envelope, Gracie went to the front of the shop and slipped a packet of everlasting seeds into the bag for Pierre.

SHE HOPED GILBERT WOULD COME AGAIN SOON, and that he might stay longer than the last time. She was so often alone, though she didn't have time to be lonely. School and the shop kept her busier than she ever wanted to be.

In rare free moments, she visited Peggy Maunder and together they planned their escape from St. Helena.

"When I'm sixteen, I'll leave home," said Peggy. "I'll stow away in a sailing ship."

"What will you take to eat?"

"Dried fruit and nuts and coconut... and lots of water."

"How will you carry it?"

Peggy giggled. "I'll get you to help me."

They sat side by side with their feet dangling over rocks beside the quay. "Three more years," murmured Gracie. "Can we wait that long? But I don't think I'd like sixty-seven days without a wash."

"Hester's ship stopped at all these places on the way— Ascension Island and Africa and an island with a bird name... Canary, I think. What would we do there?"

They stared at the sea, hardly noticing the waves that slapped against the rocks. Peggy's ginger hair hung in ringlets down each side of her face. When she needed to think, she tugged on one ringlet, as if it might get something started. This time, it didn't work.

"Looks as if we'll be stuck here forever," she said.

"Mmm," murmured Gracie. "But I'm saving. I won't give up hope."

"What will we do about our parents?"

"That's the trouble," said Gracie. "I don't think Father could manage without me." Getting away from St. Helena was a very serious business.

They sat and watched the residents passing by. Apart from the soldiers and sailors, nobody was a stranger to them. Everyone nodded, waved or said hello. Gracie found herself looking up each time the light flickered across the path. A long, slanting shadow hovered for a moment, then moved on, but in that second Gracie had seen the soldier's face.

Without thinking, she jumped to her feet and ran after him. "Excuse me, excuse me..."

The soldier turned around.

"Oh, it's all right," she said, suddenly timid.

"What's wrong, child?"

"I... I thought you were somebody else."

He bent towards her. "Do I look like someone you know?"

"No, not really."

"That's all right," he said. "I have a very common face."

You're stupid, Gracie, she told herself. Now you've lost your chance. He's tall, and he's nice. It could still be him. She stood, staring at the sea, but not moving away. She mustn't let him go, not yet.

She summoned up her courage. "You're not... you wouldn't be Isaac Taverner?"

"Why do you ask?"

"It's nothing, I just thought..." She looked up at him. "You're not, then."

He shook his head. "No, but I knew him. We were together, fighting the French."

"He isn't here, is he?"

"I'm afraid not. Isaac was killed eight years ago, in Spain."

"Dead," murmured Gracie.

"Sorry," said the tall soldier. "Did you know him, then?"

Gracie turned away. "No, no, I didn't."

Peggy ran up to her and took her hand. "Hurry up, Gracie, what's wrong?"

"I'm not sure," said Gracie, but she understood a lot more now.

WHENEVER GRACIE HAD DONE ANYTHING BAD, guilt made her rude and grumpy. Hiding her shame made her even worse. How could her father bear the shame of having run away, causing his brother to go to war instead of him? She had no idea how long it would have taken for Samuel to get word of Isaac's death, but she felt sure he knew. He'd kept it to himself, and told no one, except, perhaps, Rose.

"Father," she said that night. "I talked to a soldier today."

Samuel dropped the papers he was holding. "You take care, Gracie."

"He told me something."

Samuel's cheek twitched as he watched her face. "Go on."

"He said... he knew your brother Isaac."

Samuel sat down, and waited for her to continue.

"Father, why didn't you ever tell me?"

"Tell you what, Gracie? What else did this soldier tell you?"

"Only that Isaac had died in the war."

"Yes," said Samuel. "Yes." He slumped on the stool.

"If you'd told us, Father…"

His voice was flat, as if all his strength had drained away. "What would you have me say?"

"Just so we knew what had happened, and we'd understand."

He shook his head. "No, you wouldn't, because Isaac should never have been in the army. It should have been me."

"I'm glad it wasn't," said Gracie.

Samuel looked up, wearily. "Thank you, Gracie."

But she hadn't finished with him yet. "Father, remember when I was six and I ate all that butterscotch?"

He grunted. "What's that got to do with it?"

"I couldn't stop myself. And when you asked, I said it wasn't me, it was the rats. I was horrid to you and Mama for a whole day, because I felt so bad about it. You're like that, Father."

He stared at her, then sighed, as if he understood.

"Guilt does terrible things to a man, Gracie. I know I haven't been nice at times."

"Yes." There, she'd said it.

"Imagine how my parents felt, losing both their boys—especially their favorite. I turned my back on them, but I didn't know Isaac would go into the army. He wanted to be a doctor. If I'd stayed, and become a soldier…"

"You didn't even tell me I had an uncle. And what about my grandparents?"

"I don't know. We lost touch. They're old now, and wouldn't want to know me." He stared at his hands, then turned to Gracie. "You miss your parents, you know."

"Yes," she said softly.

When Samuel stood up, he looked so small. "It's time we

thought about dinner." He fiddled with a pan on the stove, as if his mind was not on cooking. "Who was this soldier? What was his name?"

"I didn't ask. But I'll know if I see him again."

"Good. I'd like to talk to him."

Dear Hester

You haven't missed anything. The shop is busy, the soldiers are still here, but Bonaparte never comes to Jamestown.

Some of my everlasting seeds have sprouted. I checked them every day and it seemed like weeks before one appeared and then a few more. They have spindly leaves and nothing like a flower bud.

Remember your parents telling me about Father's brother Isaac? What I want to tell you is I don't have an uncle after all. I met this soldier in the street who told me Isaac had died in the war. Father was calm when he realized I knew. He was relieved, I think, that he could share the burden, but now he has his mind set on only one thing. He wants to meet the soldier—but I hadn't asked his name!

I don't know what the soldier can tell him, or what difference it will make, but Father is determined. It's suddenly so important to him. I suppose it's been important all along, but he wouldn't say so. He went to the barracks and asked, "Do you have a tall soldier who knew Isaac Taverner?" I mean, they're not going to bother, are they? So he's started roaming the streets and now, instead of turning away from the soldiers, he stares at them and tracks them down. He stops every tall soldier, "Excuse me, I'm Samuel Taverner." I bet they think, "So what?" But they're all polite, and say, "Sorry."

I didn't ever believe there were so many tall soldiers! I'll write again,
     Love, Gracie

1818

18

GRACIE HEARD THE CLIP OF HOOVES outside the shop. From the upstairs window, she saw two horses, and one rider. Quickly, she brushed her hair before she ran downstairs.

Gilbert knocked on the door. Gracie turned the key in the lock. "Sorry, we're shut on Sundays!" She laughed. "But you're allowed in."

"I'm not coming in," he said. "I'm taking you for a ride."

Gracie looked at the two horses hitched to a post. "Me? Truly?"

He slapped the chestnut on the rump. "She's quiet as a mouse. You couldn't fall off if you tried."

"Where are we going?"

"I'm taking you back to The Briars."

"To see Toby!"

"He still asks about you."

It was nearly two years since she'd finished at The Briars. In spite of her intentions, she'd never been back. She wondered what her father would say, but she was determined to go now.

Samuel came to the door. "Father, you know Gilbert Proctor. We're going for a ride."

Samuel raised his eyebrows and peered at Gilbert, making up his mind about him. "You look after her, then."

"Oh, Father, I can look after myself." She could, she knew, but right now her mind was in a spin. Her thoughts flew off in different directions. Was this really Gracie Taverner, about to ride a horse to The Briars? Had Gilbert Proctor really come for *her*, Gracie?

She stepped towards the chestnut as if she were sleepwalking with her eyes open. What do I look like? I didn't brush my hair properly. I'm not wearing the right dress. She felt weightless as Gilbert legged her onto the chestnut. She didn't notice how she came to be sitting sideways on the saddle. When Gilbert handed her the reins, her fingers didn't look like *her* fingers, but she took a firm grip and waited while he mounted the gray.

Together they clattered along the cobbles towards the hills. Gracie had trodden the road to The Briars so many times, but never before been on horseback. From where she sat, the mountain of rock appeared less menacing and the air lighter on her shoulders. The friendly jig of hooves, and Gilbert beside her, made her want to sing.

"Can we do this again?" she asked.

"We've only just started," he replied.

The chestnut knew every rut in the road, and carried her carefully towards The Briars. The avenue of banyan trees looked exactly as when she'd last seen it. Only the sentry at the gate was missing. They rode through the entrance and along the path to the stables.

Children's voices drifted across the lawn, where the Balcombes were gathered with guests from the port. The marquee had gone, but Gracie could still make out the outline of a crown in the grass.

They knew where they'd find Toby. His vegetable garden was like a painting, a neat pattern of rows and squares and sticks like wigwams supporting climbing beans. Toby bent among the leaves of his melons. He stood up when he heard the click of the gate, and his face spread into an enormous Toby grin. "Miss Gracie!"

"Hello, Toby." She'd never forgotten him, but she hadn't expected to feel like this. It took a moment before she could say any more. She stood, smiling at him, noticing his old, stooped shoulders and the slow sway of his head.

"Things are good?" he asked.

She nodded. "And you, Toby?"

"Always good. I still make garden. I give you yams and beans for home."

Gracie knew that giving made Toby happy. "Thank you," she said. "But this wasn't why we came."

Toby turned to Gilbert. "You go to Longwood now?"

"Not today."

It hurt to see Toby's disappointment. "Couldn't we go, Gilbert?" she asked. "Please, let's go! I haven't ever seen Longwood."

"I send beans and yams to Boney," said Toby.

"Oh, all right, I suppose we have time."

Gracie clapped her hands. "Good!" Suddenly, and for many reasons, she wanted to see the place. One of the reasons was that it would make the day last longer.

"I pick roses, too," said Toby, hobbling to the gate. In his lumbering walk, he led them to the rose arbor, where bushes drooped to the ground with white and yellow blooms.

Gilbert leaned towards Gracie, and whispered, "Toby always gives me roses to take to Longwood—prickles and all."

When they reached the stable, he fixed the vegetables and flowers in a pack across the saddle. "I'll carry them all. You don't want a thorn in your side."

Toby stood and watched as they rode down the winding drive. Gracie waved until a bend in the path blocked him from her view.

"He'll be happy for another week," Gilbert told Gracie, "now that Boney has his fresh supplies."

The hills flattened out as they left The Briars and headed towards Longwood. At every turn in the track, soldiers stood guard, their red coats a shock against the barren landscape. Wide, arid plains stretched about them, with hardly a tree in sight. Only the soldiers and wandering wild goats enlivened the wasteland.

The sun beat down on their heads. The wind blasted hot air in their faces. In spite of all she'd been told about Deadwood, she wasn't prepared for this desolation. Dust swirled across the plain. "You said you wanted to come," said Gilbert.

"And I still do."

An enormous timber fence surrounded Longwood House, with guards stationed every few steps. Bugle calls rang out from the regiment camped by the gate. To the west, redcoats manned cannons at the fortress, where Union Jacks fluttered above the huts.

Gilbert rode up to the sentry at the guardhouse. "Proctor,

from The Briars," he said. "With gifts for General Bonaparte."

Gracie heard the firm tone of his voice. She noticed his strong jaw and the rust-colored curls sitting tightly around his face. He's a man, she thought.

"Pass," said the sentry.

"How far can we go?" asked Gracie.

"As far as the fence, but no farther."

The white fence had been built around Longwood House to protect Bonaparte from prying eyes. A sentry stood to attention when Gilbert and Gracie approached. Gilbert saluted as the soldier took the gifts. "For the General?"

"Yes, from Toby at The Briars."

"Right!" The soldier saluted, and sent them on their way.

Gracie wondered if Bonaparte ever received Toby's offerings.

"I know what you're thinking," said Gilbert. "Pierre sees that Boney gets them."

"So we can't go in," she said. It was a long ride just to see nothing but dust and rock.

"I'll take you to a spot where we can look over the fence."

The long, low, wooden house, which had once been a row of cattle stalls, did not look like the home of an emperor. A lone gumwood tree, driven by the wind, lurched as if it had turned its back on the world.

"Follow me," said Gilbert, guiding the gray along the boundary to a spot where the land rose and the fence appeared lower. He pulled his horse to a stop. "Look, here, you can see what's going on inside."

Gracie drew herself as tall as she could in the saddle, and peered over the wall. "Oh!" she cried. "I thought there was nothing, but look!"

In the corner of the yard, a drift of pink shimmered in the midday sun. Everlastings! She began to laugh. "Gilbert, look! Everlastings!"

"Is that what they are?"

"Yes, yes! Everlastings!"

"Boney has started a garden. I heard that a few months ago he stopped moping around. See the paths he's laid out, the beds for flowers, and the arbor for roses!"

Gracie could see. She also saw a short, flabby figure in sloppy clothes with a red handkerchief around his neck and a big straw hat hiding his face. The man stopped digging and leaned on his spade.

"It's him!" She ducked her head below the fenceline.

"He won't eat you," said Gilbert.

"N-no, I know that. It's just that... I don't like him. I don't *think* I like him."

"But what do you make of his garden?"

"One day it will be nice."

"It's his new empire. It started with those pink flowers and since then he hasn't stopped. He isn't too well, they say, but the garden keeps him going."

"How do you know all this?"

"The soldiers tell me. Boney has all these Chinese gardeners helping him."

"Mama always told me the Chinese were good gardeners."

"Yes, well, he has other laborers, too. At five in the morning he throws a clod of soil at his servants' attic window, and calls out that it's time for work. He's at it all morning, dripping with sweat, looking as if he'll have a heart attack, making his garden."

Gracie didn't tell Gilbert that she'd had something to do with it.

He smiled as she sat back on her horse. "Seen enough?"

"I suppose so." But before they moved on, she grasped the top of the fence and pulled herself up for one last look. As she stared, Bonaparte paused and pushed his hat back on his head. When he saw her there, she looked away. But in that moment she'd seen that the gray eyes were blue and that they knew much more than she'd ever imagined.

Dear Bonaparte, she wrote that evening,
Did you know it was me who sent the everlasting seeds?

She left the letter unsigned, and stowed it in a box under her bed.

NEXT EVENING, as soon as the day's work was done, she sat down again to write.

Dear Hester,
I can't wait to tell you about a garden. No, not mine! Our everlasting seeds are blooming in Bonaparte's garden. It's hard to believe that a man like that could even try to grow things, especially here, on this island.

The groom I told you about is really nice. He took me to Longwood and I looked over the fence. It was like opening a picture book. There, suddenly, was a spread of pink everlastings. And that's not all. Bonaparte is laying out paths and beds of trees and roses and there's something that could be a fishpond.

I've seen him, too. He looks fat and old and sick. His ser-

vants still call him Your Majesty, but he doesn't look at all like an emperor. Remember, Mama used to tell me to take people as I found them. So I no longer think of Bonaparte as a monster. He's a gardener.

Love, Gracie

1819

19

THE START OF A NEW YEAR was like the turning of a crisp, new page. Gracie wanted to be new, too. Different.

She peered into the small mirror in her upstairs room and pulled her hair back from her face. It made her look older, and elegant, perhaps. She wound her hair upwards and coiled it into a roll as she'd seen the French women do. It accentuated her high cheekbones and the gentle slant of her eyes.

In her drawer, she had a ribbon. She took it out and wound it through her hair, fastening it securely at the back. And she smiled at herself.

When she walked down to the shop, Samuel's eyes blazed. "What the...!" Then he stopped. He swallowed hard.

"What do you think?" asked Gracie.

"For a moment, you looked like your mother. You *do* look like her."

Gracie smiled. "Good."

"But why... why did you do it?" He wasn't angry, after all.

"Just experimenting," she said. "I'll save it for one day when I go somewhere special." She wondered when that would be. She wished Gilbert would come again. He didn't ever tell when he was coming, and it was weeks since she'd seen him.

Samuel was growing restless, too. Gracie saw it in his eyes. He needed to talk with the soldier who'd known his brother, and he couldn't find him.

"Perhaps he's at Deadwood camp," said Gracie. "There are hundreds of soldiers on the plain."

"Hmph!" said Samuel. "How am I going to get there?"

"We'll keep looking, Father. You never know when he might come to town."

So whenever the shop was closed, she walked with Samuel, and weeks later, when they'd seen every soldier in Jamestown and she almost felt she knew them all, she saw the tall soldier walking towards them.

"It's him!" she screamed.

The soldier recognized her. He stopped and saluted.

"Do you mind talking to my father?" she asked.

The soldier smiled, as if this was a funny question. "I'm off duty. It would be a pleasure."

"This is my father," said Gracie. "Isaac Taverner was his brother."

The soldier put out his hand, then clasped Samuel's shoulder. Samuel's face was sickly pale.

"I knew your brother," said the soldier. "We fought together against Napoleon in Spain. Isaac was a good soldier."

"He should have been a doctor," murmured Samuel.

The soldier looked around. "Can we sit down some-where?"

"Come to the shop," said Samuel. "It's just around the corner. I'll make some coffee."

They sat at a table in the back room with the CLOSED sign on the shopfront. "You haven't been home for a long time?" the soldier said.

Samuel shook his head. "Nineteen years."

The soldier put down his coffee cup and looked into Samuel's eyes. "So you didn't know, then? Your brother *was* a doctor."

Samuel dropped his spoon into the saucer, and stared at the spill on the cloth before he raised his head. "No, no, I didn't know."

"He was a doctor *and* a soldier."

"I lost touch," said Samuel. "We were twins, you know."

Now, thought Gracie. I'll find out things I've always wanted to know.

"I never would have made a soldier," Samuel went on. "But I thought my brother had been pressed into taking my place."

"I met your parents," said the soldier.

My grandparents, thought Gracie.

"If I'd known they had a son on St. Helena, I would have looked you up."

Samuel didn't answer, and Gracie knew that his parents hadn't told the soldier they had another son.

"I went to their house. It's a pretty village, Limpsfield."

Samuel nodded. "How were they, my parents?"

"As well as could be expected. Proud, they were... and coping. They went to the ceremony to accept his medal. He was the bravest medico in the field; took the gunfire himself to save a soldier's life."

"I never knew that," said Samuel.

"A letter takes a long time, I understand. In the end, you give up writing home."

"I never started," said Samuel. "I ran away, you see. I've been carrying that on my back ever since. And Gracie here, I've made her pay for it, too."

The soldier coughed and stood up. "Thanks for the coffee. If I can fill you in on anything, you'll find me with the 53rd Regiment. I never thought I'd end up here, watching over the mighty Napoleon. He's a shadow of what he once was."

When the soldier left to return to camp, they still hadn't asked his name. Samuel stood at the shop window and watched him walk away, straight and tall like his brother had been.

"I wonder whether they ever think of me," he said.

"They? Who?"

"My parents."

"Of course they do."

"Yet they don't speak of me."

"Well..." said Gracie. "Then why don't you write?"

"I just might," he said.

Dear Hester,

You won't believe this! We found the soldier! A load like a great sack has lifted off Father's shoulders—all because I stopped a soldier in the street. He'd never known his brother died doing something he'd chosen for himself. I kept thinking, but he's still dead. Yet somehow, it made a difference, knowing how he died. I'm telling you this—and no one else—but last night I saw Father writing a letter. I know it was to his parents. I try to picture their faces, my grandparents' faces, when they read the letter. But I don't know what they look like! Imagine

how they'll feel—after nineteen years—when they hold his let-
ter in their hands. Do you think they'll forgive him for turning
his back on them? I think so, for the thread between families
can stretch very far, and never quite break.

I put my hair up last week and it didn't look bad at all,
though not as nice as yours if you brushed it up that way. I felt
a little bit French, but didn't have the gown to go with it—or
anywhere to go. Have you?

Love, Gracie

"JANUARY THE FIRST," mused Samuel. "And we're up bright and early, the same as every other day."

"It *is* the same as every other day," said Gracie.

"Suppose you're right. But sit down, and I'll make us a special breakfast." He took down a frying pan, and eggs from the shelf. "I have some bacon with the eggs today. But no, don't sit down yet! You can make the toast." He opened a big terra cotta pot and cut two rough slices from a loaf of bread.

While he fried the bacon and eggs, Gracie held the bread in front of the fire on a long toasting fork.

"Time was, back in England, when I'd be up all night on New Year's Eve," he said. "You get older and wiser, I suppose."

"There's nowhere to go here. What did you and Mama do?"

He shrugged. "Nothing much. We lit an extra candle."

"Not even when you were young, when you first met?"

"Rose was always too busy running her parents' shop—*this* shop." He put two plates on the table. "Come on, sit down now."

"What were they like, my grandparents?" asked Gracie.

"I didn't ever meet them. They came here as laborers and never knew anything but work. They worked themselves to death before I knew them. Rose was just a young girl, struggling on her own in the shop."

It wasn't fair, thought Gracie. Only now, after two generations, had their work been rewarded.

"History repeats itself, Gracie," said Samuel. "And I won't let it!" He smiled at her. "She was so pretty, your mother, and always cheerful, kind of soothing."

"Yes," said Gracie. She rolled the jade bracelet around her wrist. The smooth stone was cool against her skin.

"Rose didn't want you to have to work like she did. She wanted you to have some joy in your life. I haven't seen to that. I've let her down."

It was strange, thought Gracie, but hearing her father talk like this almost *was* like joy to her. "It's all right, Father," she said.

He watched her fingering the jade bracelet. "That's all you have," he murmured, and left her sitting at the table.

Gracie waited, thinking she should get up and clear away the dishes. Had she offended him again? She heard him in the bedroom, the clink of a wardrobe door and the grating of drawers. Something must have upset him. He'd walked off, just as she felt she was getting close to him.

For a moment, there was silence. Then Gracie saw his face at the door. He paused before he came to the table, and held out his hand. "Gracie, do you remember this?" It was a silk rose, hand-painted in purest red.

"The day you put your hair up, I knew then I should give you this."

Gracie took the rose that her mother had worn in her hair and laid it on the table in front of her. Without a mirror, she swept her hair back from her face and swirled it around her head.

"Wear it, Gracie," he said. "It makes me feel good."

She smiled uncertainly as she set the rose above her ear and fastened the clasp.

Samuel nodded. "It's not worth anything. But it *is*. You and I know it is."

They sat facing each other across the empty plates, unwilling to move. "It's lucky we are in many ways, Gracie," said Samuel. "When you think what that soldier told us. Take Napoleon Bonaparte. When the mighty fall, they have a long way to go. And here we are, ordinary people in our own house the same as every other day, just like you said."

Except, thought Gracie, it wasn't quite true. Things *had* changed.

Dear Hester,

I write letters to you in my head, but you don't get to see them! Mama would say that's the lazy way, so here's one in pen and ink that will leave on the next ship.

The year is passing slowly, but not as horribly as in the past. Father hasn't received a letter yet from his parents, but he seems content to have made the effort himself. He's so much easier to be with that I hate to think of a reply that might upset him. For the first time, he's talked to me of Mama. At last I have a picture of her before the time I can remember. And he likes talking about her—she's part of his life again now.

But don't talk about my everlasting seeds. In the end, I

gave up. They were pathetic, weedy plants that straggled over the side of the cask and only one had a flower. It was such a strain for the poor thing that it died the next day. Everlastings are wildflowers and need to grow free, not imprisoned in a pot. Still, I thanked Father for the thought.

Gilbert and I have ridden to The Briars and Longwood again. Bonaparte's garden now has an avenue of peach trees, a walk of passionflowers, roses, a fishpond and fountain, an aviary and even a little bridge. I saw peas and beans in a corner of the vegetable garden. I'm sure Bonaparte won't let Toby know he has his own beans now.

But Hester, Bonaparte grows sicker and sicker. I've heard whispers he's being poisoned. Gilbert says he spends most of his days on his bed, and his servants help him into the garden so he can see what he's created. I peeped over the fence and saw him sitting there in a dressing gown, staring into the fishpond. He didn't look up. I thought sick people grew thin, but he gets fatter and flabbier, not a bit like the conqueror of Europe. When he arrived—was it five years ago?—he looked just like Father. Now he's an old man, as if his days have passed, and Father looks younger, brighter, ready to keep on. Sometimes it seems to me that as Bonaparte's energy saps away, Father takes on some of his strength. It's true in one way because, since Bonaparte arrived, our shop has doubled, tripled, quadrupled—more than that, but I don't know the words for five or six times—its sales. Business is so good that I don't think Father will ever leave.

So is this a happy letter? Not quite. I won't be truly happy till I get to London.

Love, Gracie

1821

21

GRACIE SHIFTED HER LEGS under the wooden desk. She'd
be glad when her schooldays were over. She was too tall now
to be sitting at this cramped table. As she jiggled on her seat,
her knee bumped the desk and upset the pen in the inkwell.
She picked it up quickly and wiped the blotch with her handkerchief.

The boy behind her kicked the back of her seat. "I saw!"

Next to her, Jess giggled.

Gracie put her head down and tried to ignore them. She'd
be in trouble again. Already, Mr. Marchant had given her extra work for not sitting up straight. The small schoolroom was
stuffy, and the warm afternoon made her yawn. Mr. Marchant
said she was lazy, when she was just tired. Now he was talking
mathematics, and square roots made no sense to Gracie at all.

"I'll never be good at this," she whispered to Jess. Adding up
shillings and pence in the shop was bad enough. She'd rather spend her last few months of school reading *Robinson Cru-*

soe or the history of England. When I grow up, she thought, I'll never be a shopkeeper or anything that requires working with figures. Samuel had promised she could be whatever she wanted to be, and perhaps she'd become a writer. She liked writing letters. Words were a passport out of here, if only in her mind. She could arrange them and rearrange them to take her anywhere. She could use her imagination with words and no one could say she was right or wrong—not like that work on the blackboard, where there was only one correct answer.

"Grace Taverner, you're dreaming again!" Mr. Marchant pointed the chalk at her.

Gracie nodded. Her mind had been a long way from the blackboard. Mr. Marchant towered over her desk. "Where were you, Gracie?"

"Oh!" She'd tell him almost the whole truth. "Just for a moment, I wasn't here." She was wondering what she'd wear in a small English village on this May afternoon.

Mr. Marchant picked up the bell from his desk. "It's time." He handed the bell to Gracie. "Here, go outside and ring the bell. It might help you to wake up."

The sound of the heavy bell tolling across the cobbled schoolyard drowned the slap of horses' hooves along the street. Gilbert waved as he rode towards her on the gray.

It took both hands to hold the bell. Gracie shook her head at him, and turned to go inside. "I only want to tell you something," he called.

He was still there, standing beside the horse, when she came outside with Peggy and Jess.

"Is that your friend?" said Peggy, and pulled Jess away. "Let's go home."

"You didn't bring a horse for me," said Gracie.

"They're all in use today. I just came to tell you, I know where Boney got those everlasting seeds."

Gracie's neck prickled. "How?"

"Toby told me. Pierre has been to see him, and Toby knows everything that goes on."

"So?"

"So I like what you did."

"Thanks."

He leaned towards her, till she could smell the soap he'd used to shave that morning. "And Bonaparte liked it, too."

Gracie looked away. She patted the horse's neck.

"The everlastings are starting to bloom again."

"Good."

"Gracie, Bonaparte wants you to see his garden."

"You're joking with me!"

"Truly, he does. Pierre has asked me to take you."

Gracie held tightly to the horse's reins. "When... when can we go?"

"How about tomorrow?"

"But it's Saturday."

"Just once, can't your father let you off?"

"We're so busy in the shop," she said. "Especially Saturday mornings."

"Then why don't I come after lunch? Surely, he'd give you an afternoon off."

"We'd be so late home. It would be dark."

Gilbert smiled at her. "I don't think I'd mind."

"All right," she said, gazing at the horse's neck and not at him. "I'll ask. I'd like to see the everlastings again."

May 5, 1821

22

GRACIE HEARD THE SCRAPE OF WHEELS outside the window and went on serving a customer. When she looked up, Gilbert stood at the door.

"Gilbert! I didn't hear the horses."

"Come and look," he said, standing aside to let her pass.

"Oh, Gilbert!"

"Not quite a carriage," he said. "But it's a start."

Samuel stepped outside and looked over the two horses. "A buggy, eh?"

"I've borrowed it, just for today. You can spare her, then?"

"Not really," said Samuel. "But she's talked me into it."

"Just this once," said Gilbert. "And never again on a Saturday."

"You'll drive it carefully, then. Those paths are mighty rough in parts."

"I know the way well," said Gilbert.

"Of course. It's just that a father worries." He ran his hand over the wheel. "I suppose it's safer than riding."

The horses tossed their heads, as if impatient to be off. Gracie tied her bonnet under her chin and gave her father a hug.

His eyes were anxious as he said goodbye. He sighed. "Go on, then. Get on with it."

Gilbert put out his hand to help her, but Gracie jumped over the wheel to the wooden seat.

"It gets a bit bumpy along the way," he said.

"That'll be fun."

He lifted his finger and tipped the bonnet back from her face. "That's better."

"Why?"

"Why wear that thing so I can't see your eyes?"

"I don't think bonnets were invented for that," she said.

He laughed at her puzzled face and the dark hair that straggled from under the bonnet. "We'll go straight to Longwood to see the everlastings. Do you know, in France they call them *immortelles?*"

"I like that word," she said.

The afternoon felt like honey around her shoulders. The wind had died and a waning sun lit up the black mountain ahead of them. Gracie felt the roughness of Gilbert's jacket against her arm. He smiled down at her. "How do you like it?"

She couldn't think of the words. She wanted so badly for them to be the right ones. "I'll tell you later," she said.

The buggy jolted over a rut in the road.

"Tell me now," he said.

"It's wonderful. Can I take the reins for a while?"

He pretended shock, but relented. "After we pass The Briars, I'll let you have a turn."

"Can't we go there first?"

"Not today. We don't have time to stop, but we'll come again."

Now and then, Gilbert pulled the buggy off the track to let a farm cart pass, but most of the time the road was empty, allowing the horses space to step out keenly towards home.

"They don't know yet that we're going to Longwood and back before they get any oats." He laughed and touched Gracie's arm. "Now, how do you like it?"

She didn't need to answer. The day had a special feel about it. Gracie didn't know what was going to happen, but she felt it would stay with her for the rest of her life. She sat beside Gilbert, and liked it. Yet there was something more than this, something she couldn't understand.

They passed the avenue leading to The Briars, and headed along the rough path towards Longwood. Gilbert pulled the horses to a stop and turned to Gracie. "All right now, change places with me." He shifted on the seat and helped her across in front of him. He handed her the reins. "Hold them like this, and just give the horses their heads. They know the way."

Give the horses their heads. It was a funny way to teach someone to drive a buggy. Gracie gritted her teeth as the horses moved away, but their strides were sure and not once did they stumble or veer off course. She soon found she could relax and turn her mind to other things.

"You're very quiet," said Gilbert.

"I was just thinking, I'd like to see Bonaparte."

· "I thought you might be thinking of me."

Her words poured out in a jumble. "Oh, well, I am, I do. It's just that I want... I'd like to tell Bonaparte that I think his garden is something special. But you know, I've never spoken to him, and I never will."

"Maybe today," he said. "If he's well enough, he might be in the garden."

Gracie shrugged. "I never told you, but I once made his bed."

Gilbert laughed. "Girls remember funny things."

As the sun slipped lower and the road grew rougher, Gracie became aware that something was happening. Close to Longwood, they heard voices, someone screaming in French and the sound of wailing.

Shouts of joy rang out from the camp. "We're leaving! Leaving! It's true!" Red-coated soldiers were waving, leaping in the air and running from their posts. The sentry box outside Longwood House was empty.

When a cannon fired, even the air seemed in turmoil. A herd of wild goats, confused by the disturbance, raced across the track in front of the buggy. Gilbert grabbed the reins, but too late. The horses reared and jerked to the side of the track. Stones crumbled under their hooves. The buggy veered into the rough. A wheel lurched over the verge, and as the horses lost their footing the buggy tilted and hurtled over the edge.

Gracie's screams were smothered by the crash of flying rocks, the strangled snort of horses and the crack of split timber as the buggy tumbled down, down to the bottom of the valley.

The last thing Gracie remembered was Gilbert reaching out to take her hand.

GRACIE DIDN'T EVER KNOW HOW SHE GOT TO JAMESTOWN. When she woke up in the hospital, Samuel was beside her. His face was white and he didn't look young any more. "I never should have let you go," he said.

She tried to argue, but her voice would not obey her mind.

"Where's Gilbert?" she asked.

"He'll be all right. You can see him soon. Shh, now."

She closed her eyes.

It was perhaps several days later, and Samuel was still there. "We're leaving here, Gracie. As soon as you're better, we're going. There'll be ships leaving, lots of them. All the soldiers are going home. We've done well the last six years, and all that's finished now. We'll go."

All the time he was speaking, she saw the figure, blurry at first, then tall and clear behind him. One arm lay in a sling, but his face was unmarked and smiling at her as he stepped towards the bed.

"Gilbert!" She tried to lift her arm.

He put out his hand and held hers against the sheet. "Me, too," he said. His voice was softer, gentler than before. "I'm leaving, too. We'll ride the streets of London together, as we always said. Would you like that?"

She wanted to say, Thank you, Father, and Yes, yes, please, Gilbert! But all she could say was, "Why?"

"Because Bonaparte is dead."

23

SO IT HAD ENDED. Gracie lay in the hospital bed as one day drifted into another, and only the rain outside the window told her that weeks had passed.

She was learning to walk again. The doctor told her she might have a limp. Her right leg had been badly crushed. But she was lucky, he said. Her ruptured kidney was healing well. She was a fit and healthy young woman.

Young woman! I suppose I am, she mused. Of course, I am! She'd known it, and now other people noticed, too.

Samuel came every day, sometimes two or three times. Gracie recognized his footsteps in the corridor, and the slight pause outside the door while he fixed a smile on his face. He wouldn't let her see his worry, but he couldn't hide his exhaustion. All the work was his alone, while she lay there, doing nothing.

"Not long now, Gracie. We'll be on that ship and all this will be behind us." He didn't mention that after a full day in the shop, selling off stock and tidying shelves, he stayed up half the night packing their own goods so they could take the first available passage to London.

Gilbert came, too. She kept a mental count of the times—five, or was it six? Almost every week, once his arm came out of the sling and he could borrow a horse. It was perhaps the seventh time, when he found her walking up the corridor, that he ran to her and swept her into his arms.

"Yes!" he cried. "You're better, I knew it! You'll be out of here, when?"

"Tomorrow." She smiled. "I'm a healthy young woman, did you know?"

He blinked as if surprised, but the jiggle of his rust-colored curls gave away his grin. "There must be a ship not far off, now. Our names are on the list—yours, your father's, and mine."

"What will you do there, in England?" she asked.

"Anything. There are so many jobs with horses. My parents have agreed, there's no future for me here." He took her hand and they walked together to the ward. "England is the place for us."

Us. Lately, she'd noticed she was reading so much into people's words. She needed to be busy again, so she didn't just laze around, thinking. She sat on a chair while Gilbert perched on the end of the high bed.

"I won't be sorry to leave the island," she said. "But there's one thing we didn't finish."

"I know. But I won't be taking you to Longwood again."

"Tell me what happened."

"There isn't much to tell. Everybody left. You heard the

commotion. The soldiers broke camp that very day. *That* day. But there were two thousand troops at the burial."

"Where?"

"Close to Longwood, at Geranium Valley. They put him in four coffins, all sealed with lead—so he couldn't escape, I suppose."

"That isn't funny."

"No, sorry."

"So what about Longwood House?"

"It's empty. The French have gone."

"And the garden?"

He shrugged. "Who knows! I don't think anybody cares. Everything's changed since... since that day. The soldiers have gone. You won't recognize the town when you get out of here."

Gracie lifted her head and fixed determined eyes on his face. "Gilbert, before we leave the island, I want to see the tomb."

"Your father might have something to say about that."

"I don't mean in a buggy. I'll be able to ride. You said I couldn't fall off the chestnut, even if I tried."

"But what's the point? It's only a grave."

She frowned at herself. "I don't know, really. Perhaps, so I can make myself believe it. Once we sail, I'll never set foot on this island again. You know I never like to leave things unfinished."

"Oh, all right," he said. "You can talk me into anything."

SAMUEL FUSSED OVER HER, and tried to protect her from strain.

"I'm perfectly healthy, Father. It's work that kept me fit, that's why I recovered so well." She flung out her arms to steady herself as she whirled in a circle. "See, I can do anything!"

He was coming to know her better. "So what is it you're getting at, Gracie? What else do you want to do?"

She laughed. "I'm only warning you, Father, because I know what you'll say. But don't worry, I'll be all right—and I'm going to do it, anyway."

"Do what?"

"Gilbert and I are going to visit Bonaparte's grave."

"What on earth for?"

"I just want to see it. Father, don't try to stop me. Don't ask any more. I can't explain."

"You're a stubborn girl, Gracie." He gave a grudging smile. "A little bit like me, I suppose."

"I won't go without telling you."

Samuel gave up the argument, and dragged a big wooden trunk into the center of the room. "There's a ship due any day now. You never know, we may be off before the end of the month."

Gracie wondered when Gilbert would come. She wanted to show him how well she could walk. Why, she could almost run! The days he didn't come passed slowly, and surely contained more hours than twenty-four. How strange it would be on the ship, seeing him every day. Or, she supposed she would. It was hard to imagine sixty-seven days on a small sailing ship. She hoped she wouldn't be seasick. Samuel had said it would be cramped and uncomfortable.

Hester had written of boredom and seasickness and gray-black waves breaking over the side. But Hester had forgotten the trials of the long voyage quickly, just as Gracie had forgotten the pain of the buggy crash. Once the trip was over, she would forget the hardship, especially when she saw Hester again. Gracie hoped Hester would come from Newcastle to see her, and soon. London was such a big place, with five hundred times as many people as the whole island of St. Helena. How could you ever find anyone in such a crowd?

Gracie tried to busy herself in the shop, but supplies on the shelves were dwindling, and customers didn't come. Jamestown had an air of doom about it. Its brief years of prosperity were over. Gracie could hardly remember life before Bonaparte, but it could never have been as dull as this.

When Gilbert finally came, she couldn't believe she'd only been home from hospital for eight days. He patted the chestnut and checked the girth strap on the sidesaddle. "She's older and slower than ever, so she'll give you a smooth ride," he told Gracie.

Gilbert and her father were still treating her as if she were sick. "I'm perfectly fit," she said, and urged the chestnut on, not waiting for Gilbert to mount the gray.

She knew she was on this path for the last time. She must open her mind to the rough track and the mountain of rock ahead, so she wouldn't ever forget the place. "There's one more thing," she told Gilbert. "I haven't asked if we could say goodbye to Toby."

He didn't answer.

"Can we?"

Gilbert turned in the saddle. "Toby isn't well."

"I can't leave without saying goodbye."

He shook his head. "I'll tell him. He'll be pleased for you, to know you're leaving."

She pulled her horse alongside the gray. "Gilbert, why can't I see him?"

"Toby's old. He feels there's nothing for him now. He's given up the garden. In the past month, I've only seen him outside once, tending the crown in the grass."

"I know what you're telling me," said Gracie. She didn't speak as they rode past the avenue of banyan trees without stopping.

It was another hour to Longwood. The grave lay in Geranium Valley, under the clump of willow trees Bonaparte had planted himself. Gracie and Gilbert dismounted and clambered down a steep path. There, beside a stream, lay a simple stone slab, surrounded by an iron railing.

Gracie stepped closer. "Oh, Gilbert, is this Bonaparte's grave?"

"You know it is."

"It doesn't say so." She leaned against the iron rail and peered at the headstone. "All it says is *Here lies...* It could be anyone," she murmured. "Why? How could they?"

Gilbert stood beside her, with his hands on the rail. "Because the French wanted the name Napoleon. And the English governor wouldn't allow it, unless Bonaparte was added. So they left it like this. No name."

Gracie shook her head. "So far from home. And not even a name." As she stared, leaves from the willows blew over the grave and settled among dust on the slab. She looked around her at the untended grass and stunted willows. She snapped a sprig of leaves from a tree and kneeled at the edge of the grave. Using the sprig as a broom, she reached between the rails to brush away the dirt and fallen leaves.

For a moment, when she stood up to look at what she had done, she was back in Mr. Porteous's boarding house. But this time, she hadn't been ordered to do it. And she'd leave no note behind. She touched the rose in her hair, but knew this must always belong to her. Across the valley, a small splash of red glinted in the grass. She picked a wild red geranium and laid it on the stone slab.

"Come on, now," said Gilbert. Gently, he pulled her away. "You can't do any more."

When they were nearing Jamestown at the end of a long day, he stopped, overlooking the port. "I didn't tell you before, but there's a ship outside the harbor."

"Then we'll be going home."

Nineteen years later

THIS LETTER WAS FOUND in a small box left on the steps of the Hôtel des Invalides, Paris, on the evening of December 15, 1840.

Dear Napoleon,

I wanted to be here today, and I wanted to bring our daughter. We came across from London, Josie and I, to see your return to Paris. She's only twelve and she knows so much about you. Her father and I have told her.

History says that after that first night on St. Helena, you never set foot in Jamestown again. I know better. I know you made a special visit, just to help me. Because of you, the island prospered for a while. And because of you, we left. You freed me, and Father, too. Imagine how I felt leaving that island, knowing you were lying there, and they hadn't even put your name on the stone slab. For nineteen years you lay in an unmarked grave.

So we came to Paris. And we stood in the Avenue des Champs-Elysées, with people who had flocked from all over France to see you come home. You didn't hear the cannons firing as your coffin came past on the huge gilt carriage. Over and over again, they fired. You didn't see your old Imperial Guard and all those Generals marching behind the carriage. People cried, but they cheered, too. It was a victory parade, not a funeral. "Vive l'Empereur!" they shouted. Long live the Emperor!

And now, you're lying under the big dome of Les Invalides, by the river Seine as you always wanted.

Tomorrow, Josie and I will return to London. Gilbert will be there to meet us, and Father as well. He's living down in Limpsfield near my grandparents—as if you need to know this! All of them, and Hester, too, will be waiting to hear, waiting for me to finish off the story.

It has a happy ending. None of us are prisoners now.

SIGNED: *Grace Proctor*

Also by Errol Broome

About the author

ERROL BROOME GREW UP IN PERTH. After a career in journalism she turned to fiction writing and has published many books for children. When writing *Gracie and the Emperor* Errol had to find a balance between truth and fiction. The Emperor Napoleon is the most written about person in the world, but Gracie is a figure of Errol's imagination.

Errol was fascinated by the impact Napoleon's arrival must have had on residents of the small island community of St. Helena. Her great-grandparents, Frederick Moss and Emily Carew, lived there. Frederick was born in the Longwood house that had been intended for Napoleon. A scribbled note written by one of Errol's family tells that at the age of thirteen Frederick fell asleep on guard, while Napoleon's body was being escorted from its burial place to the dock for shipment back to Paris. As Errol read through family cuttings and letters, she felt as if something of those momentous days had passed on to her. Although she has never been to St. Helena, its mountains of rock and the whitewashed houses of Jamestown feel familiar to her.

Errol Broome won the 1992 Western Australian Premier's Book Award for children's fiction and was shortlisted for the 1992 Multicultural Children's Literature Award. A recent novel was an Honour Book in the 2001 Australian Children's Book Council awards.

Errol lives in Melbourne with her husband.

Acknowledgments

JULIA BLACKBURN'S *The Emperor's Last Island—A Journey to St. Helena* (Martin Secker & Warburg, 1991) is a most marvelous book and an inspiration to me.

For French dialogue, to Carolyn Macafee and Sophie Gammon, *merci*.

Special thanks to Edel Wignell.